DORIAN SUMPTER

Twin Roses

This book was professionally typeset on Reedsy.
Find out more at reedsy.com

For Clarissa,

my love, my compass, my calm in every storm.
You have seen me in silence and in fire, in doubt and in purpose—and through it
all, you never wavered. Your belief in me is the quiet force that moves mountains.
Your love is the warmth that fills every hollow space. When I thought I was writing
alone, you were always beside me—in every word, every hour, every breath.
This book is a piece of my soul, and my soul has always belonged to you.
Forever and always,
D.J.

Contents

Acknowledgments

Writing this book has been a journey of heart, discipline, and vulnerability—and I could not have done it without the unwavering love and support of those who have walked beside me.

To my mother, **Gloria Sumpter**—your quiet strength and unconditional belief in me have been the foundation of everything I've achieved. Thank you for always reminding me who I am and who I can be.

To my wife, **Clarissa Sumpter**—you are my heart, my constant, my home. Your love has carried me through the late nights and long pages. Thank you for being my light in every season.

To my sisters, **Kamisha Pruitt**, **Tomica Staley**, and **Brianna Gray**—you are my lifelong protectors and encouragers. Your voices echo in my strength, and your support has lifted me higher than you'll ever know.

To my daughter, **Myriam Sumpter**—your smile brightens my world in ways words cannot express. You are my joy, my muse, and the reason I believe in beauty and purpose.

To my brother-in-arms, **Torry Weatherspoon**—thank you for helping to bring this vision to life. Your loyalty, creativity, and belief in this story breathed energy into every step of the process. I am forever grateful for your camaraderie and trust.

And above all, I thank **God**—for the gifts You have placed in my hands, the courage to pursue them, and the voice to shape something meaningful. I pray that I continue to use these talents with intention and grace.

This work is not mine alone. It belongs to each of you. Thank you—from the depths of my soul.
    —D.J. Sumpter

Trigger Warning

This book contains mature themes, graphic sexual content, psychological manipulation, emotional abuse, trauma, violence, and morally complex relationships.

Reader discretion is strongly advised.

Twin Roses explores power, desire, and identity through a dark, erotic lens. It is not intended for sensitive readers or anyone under the age of 18.

Prologue

Rain fell in waves that night, warm and heavy as blood. Thunder cracked the sky in violent paroxysms, mirroring the twin cries of two infants born under the same waning moon—one in silk and wealth, the other in secrecy and sin.

In the ancestral Solé estate, Camellia Solé was delivered amid silver chandeliers and scented linens. Her mother, Vivienne, daughter of a powerful and merciless Southern matriarch, gasped her final breath the moment the child's wails pierced the room. The attending nurse covered her mouth, trembling. A life taken for a life given. The price of legacy.

Less than two miles away, hidden in a crumbling garden house behind the estate, another woman labored alone in the dark. She was the mistress—unknown to most, despised by those who did. The second child, Dhalia, came into the world bathed in shadows and silence. There were no cries, no lullabies, no warm arms—just blood, pain, and the terror of knowing she'd given birth to a bastard flower that would not be allowed to bloom.

By sunrise, the mistress was dead—poisoned by the grandmother's order, masked as a postpartum tragedy. The patriarch, Laurent Solé, arrived too late. Grief cut through him, ragged and irrational. He had lost both his women—his wife and his lover—but two daughters now existed where once there had been none.

Camellia was given the nursery and the Solé name. Dhalia was wrapped in anonymity and carried through the servants' entrance. Laurent claimed her as a distant cousin's orphaned child, insisting she grow alongside his only heir.

"I won't have them torn from one another," he told his mother coldly. "Let them grow together. They are sisters in soul, if not in truth."

The grandmother—cold as porcelain and twice as fragile—allowed it. But in secret, she vowed Dhalia would never outshine the bloom born of marriage and power.

Years passed. The girls grew—alike in beauty, but not in blood. Camellia, poised and praised, inherited her mother's ambition and grace. Dhalia, sharp-eyed and silent, learned how to move like a shadow and listen when no one saw her there.

When Laurent died suddenly, and the grandmother followed shortly after, the truth was buried alongside them in the Solé crypt.

And yet, secrets never truly die. They linger. Like perfume. Like poison. Like lust.

And when roses bloom in mirrored gardens, only one flower survives the frost.

The Solé estate aged like wine—heady, deep, and stained with secrets.

Camellia and Dhalia grew within it like vines trained by iron trellises. By twelve, Camellia was already curating her first private gallery wall with her grandmother's approval. Dhalia, uninvited, still watched every brushstroke with a sharp, almost reverent gaze.

They wore matching uniforms to school, but that was where the similarities ended.

Camellia spoke with the measured authority of a leader in waiting. Dhalia held her tongue until she chose not to—and when she did, her words bit like the cold. Teachers praised Camellia's poise, and feared Dhalia's insight.

At home, their shared hallway became a line of demarcation. On one side: Camellia's room, filled with light and ordered canvases. On the other: Dhalia's dim sanctuary, veiled in gauze curtains, books stacked like fortresses, and drawings in charcoal that often featured faces without eyes.

Camellia blossomed in the gallery's spotlight. Her confidence was performative—perfect. She thrived under attention, wielding it like a painter's knife.

But it was Dhalia who watched what others missed. The locked drawers. The whispered late-night calls. The dusty ledger in the study's upper shelf that didn't belong to any gallery inventory.

One autumn evening, they found themselves alone in the mirrored ballroom, the one no guests were allowed to enter. Camellia practiced her speech for an upcoming exhibit, her voice echoing in glass. Dhalia leaned against the mirrored pillar, arms crossed.

"You always speak like someone's recording you," Dhalia murmured.

Camellia turned, unflinching. "And you always watch like you're waiting for me to break."

They stared at one another, breath held, the air between them charged and complicated. It wasn't hate. It wasn't love. It was something stranger. Something forged in bloodlines neither fully understood.

By sixteen, Camellia had won her first gallery feature. Dhalia submitted a piece anonymously—and watched it be dismissed by Camellia without hesitation.

By seventeen, Camellia was learning to command entire rooms. Dhalia learned how to disappear from them.

What neither of them knew was that the mirror between them had already begun to crack.

And when it broke—when the truth beneath their legacy rose to the surface—it would shatter everything.

By the time they were twenty, their twin roses had bloomed in entirely opposite directions—one cultivated and adored, the other quiet and increasingly volatile. Camellia became the face of the Solé legacy. Dhalia, the forgotten understudy, spiraled into a whisper of defiance and curiosity too dangerous to ignore.

It was a fire that started the rumors.

The estate's north wing went up in flames the night after a confrontation no one else witnessed. Dhalia had cornered Camellia in the mirrored room, demanding answers—about the hidden birth record, about the gallery funds, about the legacy that didn't belong to just one of them. Their voices rose. Then the power cut out.

By morning, only ash remained of Dhalia's room. Her body was never recovered—just scorched remnants of a dress, and smoke-choked air that lingered like a curse. The coroner ruled it accidental. Camellia, with a silent scream buried in her bones, accepted the story. Publicly.

Privately, she never spoke Dhalia's name again.

But not all deaths are endings.

While Camellia buried the past, Dhalia moved into it—slipping through the cracks of systems she learned to exploit. With a name erased and a face half-known, she stitched together a network of eyes and ears across cities, across galleries, across the silence that once bound her. From the shadows, she watched Camellia become everything she was promised.

And she waited.

Waited for the moment to rise, not as a sister—but as something far more dangerous.

Chapter One: The Gallery

Fifteen years later...

Camellia Solé adjusted the thin strap of her black silk dress, the fabric clinging to her body like a second skin as she surveyed the final lighting test in the gallery atrium. Her heels clicked across marble like the ticking of a clock. Precision. Perfection. Every exhibit in place. Every guest list vetted.

Camellia always believed in the language of space—what a room said in absence more than presence. Her gallery on 3 Promenade du Belvédère—a quiet bluff overlooking the Seine, just upriver from Île Seguin. was a whisper of her control: white walls kissed with natural light, sculptures casting shadows like secrets, and paintings so carefully spaced they breathed. People called her meticulous. In truth, Camellia was obsessed with curation, with choosing what stayed and what disappeared.

By seven that morning, she'd already opened the floor, arranged the final pieces for the evening's showing, and double-checked the staff's pacing notes. She wore silk: black open-back gown and a pearl shawl that dipped low enough to hint but not offer. Her hair, in its sculpted bun, hadn't moved since sunrise. Her heels clicked against the marble like a metronome, keeping her world in rhythm.

Art was her sanctuary. Her obsession. Her weapon.

Every piece she selected, every inch of wall space left blank, was part of a silent conversation between her and the patrons who walked into her curated universe. Camellia didn't just showcase beauty—she exposed vulnerability beneath lacquered surfaces. She controlled the story. No one ever questioned the narrative she composed.

Not until now.

The day moved with deliberate grace. Floral deliveries came in waves—orchids, calla lilies, and white roses—as requested. The scent curled around the gallery's polished bones like perfume on bare skin. Lighting was recalibrated with the help of Vivianne, her poised second-in-command, and every wine glass and hors d'oeuvre tray was arranged like they were part of an installation themselves.

Camellia's favorite room—the Mirrored Room—received extra attention. Hidden behind a velvet-paneled corridor, it was her private sanctuary, a space layered in reflections. Floor-to-ceiling mirrors on all sides, mirrored ceilings above, subtle rose-tinted LED lighting that could change tone and temperature, and small embedded cameras hidden in the seams of molding—all fed to her office feed. It was where she came to be seen only by herself or by those she allowed. It was where her power could pulse, unfettered.

The door opened on a hush of wind and coffee-scented possibility. Interns shuffled in, trailed by Vivianne.

"The donor list is finalized. Press wants an early peek. And... the new intern arrived."

Camellia didn't glance up from her clipboard. "Resume?"

"Impressive. London background. Fluent in Japanese and French. Worked in restoration."

"And?"

Vivianne hesitated. "Beautiful. Too beautiful."

That got her attention.

Camellia lifted her gaze just as the intern walked in—tall, androgynous, dark hair in a careless knot, lips full and stained like crushed cherries. His name was Alex, and his eyes held the same look as a well-placed sculpture: poised to be adored. There was something practiced in his grace. Something that felt... rehearsed.

Camellia smiled. A small, tight smile that meant: I see you. I will decide how you are used.

Throughout the afternoon, guests began to arrive. The gallery swelled with the sound of jazz and soft laughter, heels on marble, and the clink of flutes.

Socialites, collectors, critics. Everyone was dressed in hues of smoke and silver, their presence curated as much as the art. Camellia moved among them like a queen hosting a ball, every gesture intentional. Behind the scenes, she gave Alex minimal instruction and watched him from corners, behind glass, in reflective metal. Watched the way he traced frames, adjusted his collar, smiled at donors. Camellia felt deep down that something was off for Alex to be a specimen so perfect. He was good, perhaps too good.

She didn't mind being seduced. As long as she retained control.

The sun dipped lower, spotlighting the sharp angles of her gallery's design. She stood near Obsidian Reverie, her centerpiece sculpture of twisted glass and steel, sipping from a crystal flute. Her nerves were steady, but her skin buzzed. Something beneath the surface stirred—a presence.

Then came the whisper of perfume she hadn't smelled in a year. Lilac and smoke. Memory and danger.

Camellia turned toward the scent.

And there she was.

Maris.

Still luminous. Still ruinous. Still the woman who had left her broken, alone and ravaged.

Her dress clung like a memory. Her smile was a blade. She didn't wave or speak. She only locked eyes with Camellia—and began to walk.

Each step punctuated the past. Maris's heels echoed louder than the murmur of guests, louder than the soft jazz humming through the speakers. Camellia's throat tightened. They hadn't seen each other since Tokyo. Since the rooftop. The rain. The lie.

Camellia couldn't think about that now.

"Camellia," Maris said. The word was a caress, but her eyes held steel.

"You're early," Camellia replied. Flat, but her fingers trembled slightly against the glass.

"I wanted to see what you'd chosen to show the world... before the lights dim."

Camellia scanned her. The subtle tension in her jaw. The hunger behind the calm. There were questions she would never ask, answers Maris would never give.

"What brings you back?"

"Art. Secrets. You."

The silence that followed was heavy with things unspoken.

"You shouldn't be here," Camellia said softly.

Maris leaned in. "And yet, here I am."

Camellia blinked—

Tokyo. One year ago. Midnight heat soaked through silk. Neon spilled across their bodies like confessions. They'd stood on the rooftop of a forgotten hotel, the city pulsing below them, the storm a promise overhead.

"You never told me why you followed me here," Maris had said.

Camellia stepped closer. "Because I wanted to see who you were without the artifice."

"And?"

Camellia had said nothing. Just reached out, pulled her into the overhang shadows. Mouth at collarbone. Hands rougher than intended. Maris didn't stop her. Maris dared her.

It was never soft between them. It was always need. Always risk.

"You don't know what you're touching," Maris had whispered.

But she had. And she hadn't cared.

Then Maris disappeared.

Now, in Île Seguin, Maris leaned closer again. "I think about Tokyo more than I should."

Their eyes locked.

But then—glass shattered.

The sound exploded from the far end of the gallery.

Guests turned.

Camellia and Maris stepped apart, startled. A frame had fallen—or been thrown. Near the west corridor stood a man not in maintenance gear, but a daring ensemble: tailored black jacket over bare chest, dark trousers, and leather gloves. His body language radiated danger, like a dancer poised to strike.

Camellia narrowed her eyes. "Who—"

9

The man's voice was smooth. "Ms. Camellia Solé. You've been asked nicely to reconsider your next show."

Maris's body shifted slightly, protective.

Alex stood behind the guests, watching. Eyes wide.

The man offered a wink, turned, and disappeared down the corridor.

Camellia exhaled. Guests began murmuring. The spell of the night disrupted.

Vivianne approached. "Should I—?"

"Clear the space," Camellia said.

Staff began ushering guests out. Camellia raised her voice gently, "Thank you all for a lovely evening. We hope tonight's art has stayed with you."

She made sure every staff member left. One by one. All but Alex.

He lingered near the corridor, uncertain. "Should I—?"

"You'll stay," Camellia said.

Maris raised a brow. Camellia met her gaze and extended a hand.

"Come."

She led them both—Alex trailing behind—through the velvet corridor to the Mirrored Room.

It smelled like roses and secrets. The lighting was low, warm, seductive. Reflections bent the space into endless versions of themselves.

Maris turned toward Camellia, voice low. "Still controlling the narrative?"

Camellia pressed her back to the mirror. "Only the ending."

Tension rippled through the room as Camellia's hand slid over Maris's wrist.

Alex watched.

Camellia turned to him. "You'll watch. For now."

He nodded, breath shallow.

Camellia turned back to Maris, slowly unzipping her dress, letting the fabric fall.

"You left me," she said.

"I had to," Maris whispered.

Camellia's fingers tightened. "Not tonight."

She pulled silken cuffs from the drawer beneath the wall panel, tying Maris's

10

wrists with the precision of a rope artist. The mirrored ceiling caught every angle. Maris was stunning and bound.

Camellia looked over her shoulder at Alex.

"Now you'll learn what it means to be mine."

And the room closed around them, breath and power suspended in glass.

The mirrored room swallowed them in silver and shadow.

Camellia entered first, barefoot now, her dress loosened at the spine but still draped like armor. The space glimmered—four walls of mirrored glass, ceiling panels fractured into angled reflections. Soft amber lighting glowed from hidden tracks, casting bodies in burnished bronze. The floor, heated and tiled in black stone, echoed with each deliberate step.

Here, Camellia was God.

From the adjacent office, a screen flickered to life, capturing every angle through discreet, inlaid lenses. She could watch everything—review every session like an artist studying brushstrokes. It wasn't just for pleasure. It was for control. For memory. For truth.

Maris followed, slower, her heels now in hand. Her dress slipped lower on one shoulder, exposing a swath of smooth skin kissed by tension. Behind her, Alex hesitated at the threshold. He still hadn't been dismissed.

"You didn't tell me to go," he said quietly.

Camellia turned, holding his gaze. "Because I want you to see."

Maris stiffened slightly. Alex stepped in, swallowed by the room's hush.

Camellia shut the door.

"Strip," she said to Maris.

A slow inhale. A flicker of resistance. But Maris obeyed.

It was a defiance in surrender, her movements full of tension. Her dress fell like spilled ink, leaving her in a delicate black thong and nothing more. Camellia retrieved silk rope from a hidden drawer beneath a mirrored bench, each length coiled like a promise.

Maris didn't ask why. She simply tilted her head. "Just this once, then."

"No," Camellia murmured. "You don't get to dictate the terms. Not anymore."

She bound Maris slowly. Expertly. Ankles to the floor rings. Wrists to the mirrored headboard. Her arms stretched above, breasts rising with shallow breaths. A visual echo multiplied across the reflective surfaces. Maris, stripped of her myth, tethered in light and shadow.

Camellia stood above Maris, the mirrored ceiling multiplying her dominance in a thousand fractured angles, every facet of her body captured in glimmering frames. Maris writhed against the silk ropes binding her wrists and thighs to the cool metal frame—her breathing unsteady, her lips parted in a silent cry that refused to fall.

"You always trembled for me," Camellia murmured, her voice molten, her fingers trailing from Maris's cheek down her neck, grazing the curve of her breast. "But tonight, you don't get to finish unless I say so."

Maris whimpered, her eyes stormy with desire and frustration. Her nipples were taut, her inner thighs slick, her body yearning for release—but Camellia didn't relent. Instead, she walked to the wall, tapped a panel, and dimmed the lights to a deep amber. Shadows licked the walls while their reflections stared back—raw, immortal, suspended in heat.

Behind her, Alex stood frozen, mouth slightly parted, his pants already strained. He didn't speak. He didn't dare.

"Watch her," Camellia commanded, turning to him without even looking. "She's yours to witness, not touch. Not unless I say."

He nodded, his voice trapped in his throat.

Camellia returned to Maris, kneeling between her thighs but never granting what Maris silently begged for. She circled her with tongue and breath and barely-there fingertips, bringing her to the edge over and over, cruel in her precision.

Then—just as Maris's body convulsed with another frustrated peak—Camellia stood. Slowly, deliberately, she walked to Alex and pulled his shirt free from his body, her fingers teasing each button until it hung open. Her dominance shifted like a second skin—fluid, commanding.

"You want me," she whispered against his ear, "but you're not getting inside me. Not tonight."

He gasped, but his hips twitched toward her.

Camellia pushed him to his knees, glancing back at Maris—bound, panting, watching with glassy, tormented eyes.

"This is your punishment," she said to Maris, loud enough for Alex to hear. "You left. And now you watch."

She lifted her dress, and guided Alex's mouth to her with a firm grip in his hair. She leaned back into the mirrored wall, her body silhouetted in refracted light, her gaze locked on Maris's as Alex moved her silk thong to the side and devoured her with reverent desperation.

And when Camellia came—hard, loud, unapologetic—it echoed through the room, mirrored and multiplied. She let her cry fill the air, her body trembling with the release she'd denied the others.

Maris sobbed—wanting, aching, broken open.

Alex knelt still, panting, lips slick, his eyes glazed in lust.

Camellia stood tall again, radiant in the afterglow, and ran a finger down Maris's cheek. "Not yet," she whispered. "You'll wait. You'll learn. You'll feel everything I decide you get to feel."

She looked at both of them, her body glowing in the mirrored twilight.

"Now, the real night begins."

Camellia paced slowly between them, her steps a rhythmic echo in the mirrored silence. Every glint of her body—her sweat-slicked skin, the flush of climax still painting her chest—was reflected around them, infinite and inescapable. The scent of sex hung thick, curling in the air like incense, rich with the memory of her release.

Maris's eyes fluttered closed, her wrists flexing against the bindings—an ache beyond the physical building in her chest. She tried not to let the tear fall, but Camellia saw it.

"I feel everything," Camellia murmured, crouching beside her, voice suddenly close, intimate. "Every lie you told. Every hour I spent wondering why you disappeared without a word. And now you do too."

Her hand traced the inside of Maris's thigh, not to arouse—but to remind.

Alex remained on his knees, his breath slowing, his lips still parted as if still tasting her. He watched, transfixed, unblinking. The room didn't feel like a gallery anymore—it felt like a shrine.

"I want her," Camellia said, gaze flicking toward him. "But she doesn't get to come until I've purged what she did to me."

Maris looked up sharply, trembling. "Cam—"

A slap—open palm, sharp across her thigh. Not violent, but commanding. Camellia's eyes darkened. "You don't speak unless I let you."

Maris's lips parted in a sob that was part arousal, part surrender. Camellia stroked the sting with her thumb.

"I'm going to let him touch you now," she said. "Only what I allow. And you're going to take it."

Maris swallowed hard and nodded.

Camellia turned to Alex, still kneeling like a supplicant. "Touch her," she said. "Just her thighs. Just enough to keep her teetering."

Alex's hands moved with reverence, sliding up Maris's quivering legs, fingers grazing the skin she craved to have claimed. Maris arched in response, but Camellia watched her face—not his touch.

She moved to the wall panel again, tapping the control for the private feed. Hidden cameras blinked to life—angles from every mirrored edge displayed now on a screen in the wall. A security system retooled for voyeurism. For control.

Camellia watched herself in a dozen frames—dominant, godlike.

She walked back to Maris and straddled her chest, hands framing her face, lips brushing hers but never kissing. Her breath was warm against Maris's mouth.

"I want you ruined," she whispered. "And waiting."

Then she stood again and pulled Alex by the hair until he gasped.

"Put your mouth on her," she said. "Everywhere but her clit."

Alex obeyed. Maris moaned, thrashing, hips bucking against the bounds. She was glistening now, pleading without words.

Camellia leaned against the wall again, watching. One hand slipped to her own breast, a lazy stroke as she took in the sight of Maris—a goddess undone, made to kneel without kneeling.

"Do you regret it yet?" Camellia asked quietly, fingers grazing herself as Alex worshipped Maris with silent devotion.

Maris bit her lip so hard it almost bled. Her eyes said yes. Her body said more.

And Camellia smiled.

Alex stood motionless. A tremor ran through him.

Camellia turned.

"Now you," she said.

He hesitated. She stepped toward him, peeled the shirt from his frame. Her hands didn't shake. She undid his belt with calm precision, every movement choreographed. When he was bare before her, Camellia guided him down to the velvet bench before Maris.

"On your knees."

The tension grew, thick as blood. The air ripe with sweat, perfume, and anticipation. Maris tried to look away, but Camellia's voice tethered her.

"No. You watch."

She took Alex in hand, controlled and slow. Her lips brushed his jaw, her voice a velvet blade.

"You came here to spy. To gather information. You thought you could control the narrative."

Alex tried to speak but Camellia shushed him.

"You don't get to speak. Not until I've taken everything I want."

Maris moaned, restrained, helpless, watching as Camellia dominated another. Her own arousal dripped onto her inner thigh, aching.

"Please," she whispered.

Camellia ignored her. She slid onto the bench, straddling Alex, grinding slow and hard. Her nails raked down his chest, drawing red lines. She pushed him back and rode him with steady, practiced rhythm—a rhythm that never broke her gaze from Maris.

Every sigh, every cry from Maris, only made Camellia grind harder. Faster. She didn't let herself come until she saw tears in Maris's eyes—not of sadness, but of thwarted need.

Then she climaxed with a cry, her body trembling, head thrown back to the mirrored ceiling.

Still seated, still pulsing, Camellia turned to Maris.

"You don't get to leave me again," she said, voice cracking from power and pain. "You don't get to haunt me and then vanish."

Maris, panting, nodded. Broken open by restraint, by memory, by want.

Aftercare came like a tide.

Camellia untied her slowly. Caressed her wrists. Held her in silence. Let Maris press her face against her shoulder.

Alex sat at the bench's edge, unsure if he was still part of this strange communion or simply its witness.

Camellia spoke without looking at either of them.

"Tonight was a reckoning. Tomorrow will be something else."

And from the office, the cameras watched. Recording everything.

Chapter Two: The Watchers

The gallery lay hushed under the weight of midnight.

The silence wasn't passive—it pressed against the mirrored walls like a held breath, thick with anticipation. Not even the distant city sirens could pierce the spell that lingered in this place. Moments earlier, it had pulsed with heat and moans, secrets and spectacle. Now, it was a church after confession.

Camellia's mirrored room still glistened with the sweat of indulgence. Ropes lay abandoned like serpents in repose, and the faintest musk of rose oil hung in the air—a signature of her presence, more potent than perfume.

The city was a veinwork of light beneath him.

From the rooftop two buildings away, a shadow crouched behind the lip of a maintenance rig, one knee pressed into concrete, silent as falling ash. The shadow was made of edges—precise, elegant, and lethal. The drone he had dispatched earlier now returned to its roost at his back—tiny, matte black, wings folding inward with insectile grace. He caught it midair and slotted it into the modular pouch at his hip. Not a sound.

Efficiency was devotion.

He remained still, watching Camellia's penthouse that was attached to the gallery from afar through infrared optics, scanning for heat patterns, electromagnetic signatures, encrypted signals. It was all here—layered, hidden like myth. Camellia's presence radiated differently. Her space wasn't just secure. It was *alive*. Conscious.

He admired that. In his own quiet way.

But admiration was irrelevant.

He blinked once, long and deliberate, activating his retinal recorder.

Playback shimmered across his cornea—frames from earlier, frozen, footage played in silence: Camellia's commanding presence filling the mirrored room, Maris gasping under her control, and Alex—disarmed, exposed, reshaped by lust and submission. The shadow slowed the feed, isolating expressions, dissecting gestures. Each flick of Camellia's wrist was measured. Each word she whispered cataloged like evidence in a sacred trial.

He didn't blink. Didn't shift. This wasn't curiosity.

Camellia tightening silk around Maris's throat, her voice soft as velvet and absolute in command. The look on Alex's face as he broke open like a prayer.

Weak. Predictable.

Still, the shadow didn't judge. He had been conditioned not to.

Emotion was… permitted only when it was useful.

This was surgical.

Data extraction.

He stood slowly, one precise movement at a time, and moved to the access point embedded in the ventilation duct. A patch of wire mesh peeled back beneath his gloved fingers. He lowered himself into the shaft with silent limbs, moving through steel and shadow.

Camellia would never hear him. That was the point.

But that didn't mean she wouldn't sense him.

And that—*that*—was what made her dangerous.

The office was dark, cooled to 67°F, optimal for machine stability and cognitive function. Minimal dust. A faint trace of clove oil in the air—a grounding agent, burned in a ritual bowl near the wet bar. Her kind of detail. Luxurious. Occult.

The shadow crouched before the console.

His breath did not fog the glass.

Gloved hands moved across the biometric override panel. His thumbprint was not a match, nor was it needed. The shadow's employer had provided him with a bypass key—planted inside the digit of a deceased operative buried beneath a hospital in Nice.

He pressed the key into the side port.

The console woke.

Light filled the room like floodwater.

Camellia's files were encrypted to the core. Still, he didn't need to break them. He only needed to see enough. To listen. To extract data and profile.

The monitors split into fifteen quadrants. Camellia on each one. Sometimes alone. Sometimes with Maris. Once—too briefly—with his employer, years ago. A security footage remnant, tucked beneath the heading *"Delphinium."*

His chest tightened.

Only slightly.

He ran a process loop to scrub for the keywords "Dhalia," "Twin," "Echo," and "Adoption." He watched the search populate, saw results shrink and vanish.

Camellia had already purged them.

She was hunting ghosts.

Good.

That meant she was looking the wrong direction.

For now.

The shadow uploaded the core files into his implant drive and disabled the monitor. He stood, eventually, sliding the drive into a slit beneath his glove and retreating soundlessly into the shadows. The room returned to darkness. As he turned to leave, he paused—just briefly—at the edge of her desk.

There was a single object sitting at its center: a fountain pen made of blackened bone, resting beside an ink blotter shaped like a thorned vine.

He didn't touch it.

But his gaze lingered.

Such deliberate aesthetic. Every piece of her office was calculated. *Sensory alignment*, his employer had called it.

Camellia designed her traps with taste.

He respected that.

Almost envied it.

The door behind him didn't creak. The lock rearmed without a sound. He disappeared like smoke in the wind.

The mirrored room below him remained still—until a breath broke the silence.The shadow turned and ghosted toward the exit.

By the time he reached the rooftop again, the city had begun to change color. Dawn painted the glass towers a bruised pink. The sounds of life resumed— sirens, buses, over-caffeinated early joggers with expensive headphones.

He activated his encrypted comm.

A woman's voice answered before the first ring finished. Not impatient— *attuned.*

"Report."

He didn't hesitate. His voice was a blade sheathed in velvet. "She's just as you described. And more dangerous than you anticipated. She's escalating."

A pause. Then, "And the boy?"

"Compromised. Emotionally. Possibly physically."

A faint hum of amusement on the other end. "She works fast."

A beat of silence. Then the woman purred.

"Perfect. Continue watching. And send me everything."

The shadow said nothing.

"She'll suspect you," his employer added, voice cool, elegant. "She doesn't believe in coincidence."

"She already suspects."

"And?"

"I let her see the frame skip."

"You left a trace?"

"Intentional. I want her alert. It makes her reckless."

Another long silence.

His employer exhaled. "You always did like pressure. Be careful, my shadow."

He didn't reply.

She changed tones—softer, rare. "I mean that."

He closed his eyes briefly. Her voice always stirred something unbidden in him.

"Understood," he said.

Then the line went dead.

The shadow stood in the wind for a long moment. He pulled his hood over his head and tucked his gloves tighter. The city below was waking up.

He was not.

He had never slept.

And soon, neither would Camellia.

Alex stood shirtless and dazed.

His chest rose and fell in sharp, ragged intervals, sheened with sweat that cooled too slowly on his skin. His trousers hung low, zipper half-undone, belt forgotten on the floor like a relic from another self. The pulse of arousal hadn't fully dissipated—it still prowled his veins like a second heart, wild and unrepentant. The mirrored chamber didn't help. It multiplied him— fractured versions of the same undone man, each reflection exposing angles of surrender he hadn't meant to show.

He rubbed his wrists.

Not because they hurt.

But because *she* had touched them.

Camellia hadn't gripped him hard. No bruises bloomed. But the imprint of her fingertips lingered just beneath the skin—like phantom cuffs made of silk and smoke. He could still hear her voice, low and unhurried, curling behind his ear like a question he wasn't supposed to answer.

He had come here wearing a mask.

Intern. Admirer. Nobody.

Sketchpad in hand. Eyes bright, posture deferential. He knew how to disappear in plain sight.

But Camellia hadn't looked past him.

She had looked *through* him.

And then she'd *peeled him open.*

Every layer he'd built, every line rehearsed, she'd undone with terrifying grace. She read his tension like notation, played it like music. She didn't seduce—she *authored.* And now her words were etched beneath his skin, sentences of submission he didn't know how to erase.

Alex sank onto the mirrored bench like a man falling from height. His hands clawed through his hair before collapsing over his face.

What the fuck had he done?

He wasn't supposed to *feel* anything. That was the first rule.

Infiltrate. Observe. Report.

And yet—

When Camellia turned her gaze on him at the end of the night—fingers tracing Maris's spine like a signature before shifting to *him*—Alex hadn't felt like an observer. Or even a pawn.

He felt chosen.

Not enlisted.

Claimed.

The way her eyes held his… like she'd always known he'd be hers.

And worse: like he'd always wanted to be.

The thought made him tremble—not from fear, but recognition. Something ancient and dangerous had been awakened in him tonight. Not lust. Not obsession.

Devotion.

A flicker caught his eye.

There was a hidden corner console—normally dead in these after-hours— buzzed to life with a soft hum. A single feed pulsed through its rotation: *Camellia's office.*

Alex straightened.

The feed rolled through static and grainy, flickering.

Then…

A jump in the timestamp.

Three seconds. Gone.

On screen, something moved. Just a shimmer too fast to register. Too precise to dismiss. A shape in the room that shouldn't have been there.

His heart jolted.

He knew Camellia's security systems better than anyone outside her private tech cadre. He'd studied the blueprints obsessively. Memorized access logs. Her office was a sanctum. Triple-coded, soundproofed, pressure-sealed. No one went in without her permission.

Not even her closest staff.

Not even Maris.

And yet…

Someone *had* been there.

His breath caught at the base of his throat, a tight pressure rising like a scream trapped in ice.

This wasn't just a breach.

It was a *message.*

Not for Camellia.

For him.

A cold ripple slid down his spine as he stared at the missing seconds on the screen. He reached for the console's rewind—fingers hesitating before pressing play again. The hairs on his arms lifted.

Because suddenly, Alex had the strangest sensation.

Not that he was being watched.

But whoever had been in that room…

Already knew his name.

Back in the penthouse bedroom above, Maris stirred.

But she wasn't asleep.

She lay curled in a tangle of silk sheets, limbs aching in the most intimate ways. The dawn light filtered through the gauzy curtains, soft and gold, tracing her bare skin like fingertips she could still *feel.* Her thighs trembled when she shifted, the muscles tender from where they'd been stretched open and held. Her lips—kiss-swollen, bruised—parted around a silent breath, the memory of Camellia's mouth imprinted like a burn she didn't want to heal.

Her wrists bore delicate red lines, barely visible now—but to Maris, they pulsed like sigils.

Marks of surrender. Of being seen.

She let her fingers drift over them slowly. Not out of concern.

But reverence.

The ache wasn't what haunted her.

It was the clarity.

Last night hadn't just been sex. It hadn't even been domination—not really. It was a recalibration of her world. A tearing down of all the boundaries she'd tried to erect after leaving. All the logic, all the reasons.

All undone.

Camellia hadn't *forced* her to fall again.

Maris had leapt.

Willingly. Desperately.

No more illusions. No more posturing. She had *begged* to be touched, *pleaded* to be owned. Every whispered command, every flick of Camellia's nails down her ribs had reduced her to pure sensation. By the end, there'd been no room for pride—only the exhale of belonging.

And the worst part?

She had loved it.

Not with the giddy pulse of new affection, but with the bone-deep ache of someone returning home to a place they swore they'd never go again.

She turned onto her side slowly, her body moving like something waterlogged—heavy with pleasure and truth. Camellia's side of the bed was empty now, but still warm, the dent in the pillow like a whisper. Maris reached out, her hand hovering there, not quite touching.

Her gaze shifted toward the sound of water being poured.

The soft *click* of a glass on the bar.

And then—barely audible—the muted thump of the office door opening and closing.

Camellia hadn't said a word.

No goodbye. No caress. No lingered glance.

Just… silence.

But Maris knew that silence like she knew her own heartbeat. It wasn't apathy.

It was control.

The kind that left her unraveling long after the ropes were untied.

Camellia never chased. Never explained. She *waited*. She knew the storm she stirred—and she knew Maris would feel it long after the lightning passed.

Maris exhaled slowly, pressing her face into the pillow.

It still smelled like Camellia's skin. Warm. Elegant. Untouchable.

God, she was unraveling.

And the worst part?

She didn't want to be stitched back together.

Not yet.

Downstairs, Camellia stood in the dim hush of her private office, barefoot, still wearing the black silk robe she'd thrown on after slipping from bed.

The room was silent except for the low hum of the wall-sized console to her right. Morning hadn't yet reached this far into the suite—no light spilled through the tall, frosted windows. It was the kind of space that always felt untouched. Too ordered. Too sacred.

She preferred it that way.

Camellia moved toward the control panel, her fingertips skimming the smooth glass. Her nails were still stained with Maris and with faint crescents of color, scent, surrender. She could still taste her if she breathed deep enough.

But her mind wasn't on the memory. Not fully.

Not anymore.

Her attention snapped to the anomaly she'd caught hours earlier just before Maris had come undone beneath her. A flicker. An error. Not enough to draw suspicion from anyone else.

But Camellia didn't make mistakes.

And her office never glitched.

She tapped the screen, eyes narrowing as the feed rewound itself in quiet increments, frame by frame. A fraction of a second dropped. The timestamp jumped. A shimmer in the corner of the camera—a sliver of shadow too deliberate to be random.

Her jaw clenched, the line of her throat tightening. She exhaled slowly, smoothing her palm over the glass as if she could force it to reveal more.

Someone had been here.

Someone had tried to be invisible.

Someone thought she wouldn't notice.

Behind her, the quiet ache of Maris's presence still clung to the air like perfume. It would've been so easy to slip back upstairs. To bury her hands in that hair, to find sanctuary in the soft cage of Maris's thighs.

But Camellia had learned long ago…

Desire was never the safest place to hide.

Not when you were being hunted.

She adjusted the lens feed, her eyes catching the briefest glitch in infrared—too low to be a trick of lighting, too rhythmic to be nothing. A pulse. A motion detector tripped. The system had tried to erase it. Which meant the breach wasn't random.

It was targeted.

Camellia smiled faintly, lips curling like a blade.

"Curious," she murmured aloud. Her voice was silk and ice. "You were watching me... but who was watching *you*?"

The smile didn't reach her eyes.

Was it the man from the gallery? It had to be.

She could feel her like a shadow at her back.

Like a twin thought buried deep.

Camellia turned her gaze toward the encrypted log. Someone had entered the biometric buffer—but there was no name, no retinal signature. A ghost.

And yet... the energy left behind wasn't foreign. Not entirely.

She tapped the console again, rerouting the system through a second layer of encryption she never used. Not unless it was personal.

Not unless it was war.

The feed shimmered, then cleared.

And there—for a blink—a silhouette.

Too tall to be Maris. Too lean to be staff.

Alex?

Her throat went taut.

No. He wouldn't dare.

Would he?

The image evaporated, pixelated beyond repair. But the question remained, cold and sharp and whispering across the back of her teeth.

Camellia stood motionless for a long moment, the silence curling around her like smoke.

Then she turned away from the screen.

Back toward the stairs.

Back toward the woman she'd left trembling in the sheets above, and back to the monitor where she saw the boy with storm in his eyes and too many secrets in his hands.

If they wanted to play, she'd let them.

But she would write the rules.

And break them—when it suited her.

Back in the mirrored room, Alex sat on the edge of the mirrored bench, trying to breathe.

His phone buzzed again.

Unknown Number: You're in deeper than you realize.

He gritted his teeth.

Then a second ping.

[Secure Channel]

Report overdue. Status update required.

Has she accessed restricted networks? Is the subject aware of our interest?

Alex closed his eyes.

They had no idea.

Camellia wasn't just aware. She was orchestrating it.

And somehow, he was becoming her instrument.

His fingers hovered over the reply. Then he deleted the message entirely.

He wasn't theirs anymore. Not really.

The scent of rose oil lingered in the room, curling around his thoughts. The knot in his gut wasn't guilt. It was longing.

He needed to see her again.

To understand.

To obey.

Hours Later…

The morning passed in a haze of porcelain clinks and quiet shadows.

Camellia sat at the sun-drenched breakfast table like a queen in a silent opera—her robe exchanged for an ivory blouse and tailored slacks, her hair swept back into a knot that made her look sharper than glass. The eggs on her plate cooled untouched. The tea had long gone bitter. But her gaze was fixed not on the food, nor the rising skyline beyond the penthouse windows.

It was fixed inward.

A slow unraveling of calculations, reactions, threads being plucked one by one until a tapestry revealed itself beneath the chaos.

Maris had said nothing when she left—just that lingering scent, the tension of goodbye unsaid. Her lipstick still marked one of the glasses, faint and intimate. Camellia hadn't touched it. Let it remain. A quiet scar.

Let her think she was choosing freedom.

She hadn't even looked back.

But Camellia had.

A glance at Maris's retreating silhouette as she slipped into the elevator. Heels echoing. Shoulders squared. Heart, Camellia knew, still raw. Still *hers*.

She returned to her office.

No more distractions.

No more indulgence.

She drew her fingers across the desk's hidden panel and summoned the projection interface. A lattice of files hovered before her—names, timestamps, coded transactions. She began a methodical review. Alex's photo flickered into view. So young. So eager. And so very unprepared for the current he'd waded into.

He'd lied, of course. But beautifully. She almost believed him.

Almost.

Camellia opened a second file. This one deeper. Older. Redacted in places only she could access. The name of the organization that had once courted her—before they realized she'd never be anyone's pawn. She'd vanished. Reinvented herself behind velvet walls and mirrors.

But they never stopped trying to claim her.

She tapped her fingers on the screen as Alex's image zoomed in: wide eyes, parted lips, the trembling precision of a man torn between duty and desire.

He had told her more with his silence than any spy report ever could.

She smiled.

Let them keep watching. Let them think they were infiltrating her sanctum undetected.

She had already started rearranging the stage.

And when the curtain finally rose—

They would kneel.

Meanwhile—Elsewhere in the City

Kenji lit a clove cigarette and waited until the encryption finished running.

The motel room was intentionally seedy. Peeling wallpaper. A flickering overhead bulb that stuttered every few seconds like a heartbeat. He'd chosen it for the irony—he always preferred beauty veiled in filth. It reminded him of his employer.

The screen brightened. Secure.

He pulled the wired earpiece in. The line opened with a soft chime.

No greeting.

No command.

She was already listening.

"Update," Kenji said, exhaling smoke in a thin stream. "He's cracked. Not all the way. But close."

A pause. Static. Then: "How close?"

His employer's voice was silk sharpened to a wire.

Kenji smirked and leaned forward, fingers dancing across the keys. A video feed appeared—grainy footage from a hallway camera spliced from an auxiliary source. The angle barely caught Alex's face as he entered the gallery's restricted wing.

"He lingered," Kenji murmured. "Watched her. Wanted her. And then?"

He queued another clip: Alex exiting the mirrored chamber hours later, shirt half-buttoned, gaze vacant, sweat clinging to his brow like regret.

"He broke protocol. Completely. No message drop. No check-in. Just..."

He tapped the screen.

"Her."

There was a beat of silence so pure it rang like a held breath.

"Camellia touched something in him," Kenji added. "Which means he's vulnerable."

"She doesn't touch unless she intends to own," replied Kenji's employer. Her voice was cool, but something quivered beneath it. Not rage. Not jealousy. Recognition.

Kenji leaned back, eyes narrowing. "You knew she'd pull him in."

"I counted on it."

Kenji let the silence stretch. "And Maris?"

"Still soft," said Kenji's employer. "Still searching for the girl she used to be." Then, quietly: "She'll break again. Just a matter of when."

Kenji tapped a key and pulled up the interior scan from Camellia's private office. "There was a breach last night. Someone got into her encrypted archive. Only a few seconds of camera drop, but she saw it."

Another pause.

"Good."

Kenji raised an eyebrow. "She's watching now. Tighter than ever. She's starting to suspect there's more than one thread in play."

"That's the point," said Kenji's employer. "She needs to feel the edges closing. Let her trace the ghosts. Let her think she's still in control."

"And when she isn't?"

A smile in her voice now. "Then I arrive."

Kenji closed the feed and ground out his cigarette. He glanced at the red threadboard on the opposite wall—photos, names, fragments of poetry, lipstick-smudged napkins.

Camellia's face was pinned dead center.

He stared at it.

At the sharpness of her gaze.

The chaos in her symmetry.

"She's going to be beautiful when she breaks," Kenji whispered.

Chapter Three: The Theatre of Control

The city throbbed like a living pulse beneath Kenji's boots as he made his way down the alley behind the old cinema. Kenji moved like vapor across the city's underbelly, tracing a path through alleys too narrow for cars and too forgotten for cameras. He adjusted the cuff of his jacket, not for vanity but to engage the micro-trigger embedded in the seam. A faint green blink. Recording complete. Neon from a broken sign above cast intermittent flashes of red across his jaw, highlighting the tension in his muscles as he reached the locked side door. Three quick knocks. A pause. Two slow. One final tap.

The door clicked open.

Inside, the projection room was cloaked in near-darkness. It was colder. Still. The stale air didn't move unless invited. Dust hung in the air like smoke. The screen below flickered with an old silent film—frames scratched, actors caught mid-expression, wide-eyed and ghostlike. A man sat near the edge, his face turned away, hair tucked beneath a midnight hood.

"You're late," he said.

Kenji didn't apologize. He stepped forward, pulling a slim drive from beneath his jacket. The chamber inside was dark, save for the flickering blue glow of a single projector. He stood in the center—his handler, shrouded in veil and shadow. No name. No title. Only a low, silken voice that melted through the silence like ink.

"Report."

Kenji knelt, not out of submission, but precision. "Target confirmed. Secondary operative compromised. Phase One engagement successful. There are… anomalies."

Kenji's handler took the drive without touching his hand. "What did you see?"

The silhouette tilted slightly. "Define."

"Camellia deviates from standard behavioral profiles. Her psychological anchors run deeper than expected. She's begun to document Alex. Not just monitor—catalog. Build patterns."

The figure didn't speak. Didn't move. The projector fed fragmented video across the walls: Camellia's performance. Alex watching from the shadows. Maris bound, trembling, radiant. A triangle unraveling.

Kenji added, almost an afterthought, "Alex isn't following protocol. He's entangled. Emotionally."

That drew a response. The figure stepped forward just enough for a glint of light to catch the bottom edge of his face. A mouth that curved into a smile. Not warm. Not cruel. Something in between. "Then let him fall."

Elsewhere, Later That Morning

Upstairs, apart from the main gallery in Camellia's penthouse, sunlight streamed in like an uninvited guest—too bright, too knowing. It spilled across the polished floor, casting long, accusatory shadows that fractured against the modern edges of art and glass. Camellia stood at the tall windows in a silk robe, her back an elegant line of restraint. Motionless. Regal. Dangerous. She didn't turn as Alex entered.

"You weren't dismissed."

The words sliced through the quiet like a blade.

His breath hitched, caught between guilt and fear, as if the sunlight itself had betrayed him.

"I—the door was open."

She turned slowly. Controlled. Deliberate.

The look in her eyes wasn't fury. It was far worse.

Calculation.

A chill bled down Alex's spine. He tried to meet her gaze, tried to summon whatever fragile courage remained in him, and failed. The memory of last night pressed down on him like a vice—her fingers on Maris, her command, her power. And him, paralyzed and aroused, a moth too aware of the flame.

"You went into my office and tampered with my security feeds," she said. The words echoed through the penthouse like a sentence handed down.

He froze. Skin cold. Every cell screaming to flee.

"No. I mean, I just saw something. In your office. A glitch."

"There are no glitches."

The silence that followed was thick with danger.

And then—movement.

Maris emerged, wrapped in a coat, her hair damp from the shower, skin still flushed from earlier, like a ghost made of longing. She paused just inside the threshold, the weight in her eyes unreadable. Her presence was quiet, but it shifted the air between them like a fault line threatening to crack.

"Leaving?" Camellia asked without turning.

No warmth. No tether.

Maris didn't answer. She looked at Alex, then Camellia, then past them both—as if already stepping into a future she hadn't decided to want.

"For now."

She walked out, each step softer than the last. Measured. Controlled. But the silence she left behind was anything but gentle.

It buzzed with everything unsaid—questions, betrayals, desire left smoldering in the ash of something neither of them fully understood.

And Camellia...

Camellia had not blinked.

On the street, Maris moved through the city like someone lost in a dream she wasn't sure she wanted to wake from. The world around her spun with motion and noise, but it felt distant—muted, like she was underwater. Her heels struck the pavement without sound, her reflection catching in store windows like a ghost she barely recognized. The ache between her thighs reminded her of everything she'd given over. Every shiver. Every whispered plea. The echo of Camellia's breath on her neck, the pressure of the silk ropes, the sensation of being... possessed.

She hated how much she craved it again.

It wasn't just memory—it was hunger. Deep. Gnawing. Alive in her blood like a fever. Her body remembered before her mind could resist. Her wrists still tingled as if the ropes had never been untied, as though Camellia's hands were still there, ghosting over her skin, claiming her inch by inch. The sensation wasn't fading—it was evolving. Lingering. Curling into something dangerously close to need.

The city didn't care about longing. Taxis splashed through puddles, a fruit vendor shouted half-hearted bargains, and the skyline held no answers. Horns blared. Shoes clacked. A woman laughed behind her, sharp and careless. Life surged on as if nothing had happened, as if Maris's entire world hadn't shifted on its axis behind velvet curtains and mirrored glass. As if she hadn't knelt willingly. Opened herself. Let go.

Maris pulled her collar up, heart pounding in her chest. She wasn't running. Not really. But she wasn't ready to admit the truth either.

She liked it.

She liked being broken open by Camellia.

And worse—she wanted more.

That realization hit like a storm in her chest, messy and electric. Wanting more meant surrender. And surrender meant returning. It meant silence, again. Control. Pleasure spun like a weapon. She stopped at a corner light, lips trembling as traffic hissed past. Rain had started, thin and cold, dusting her lashes like salt. The crosswalk flashed. She didn't move.

She stood there, trapped in a moment that felt like a decision. One she was terrified to make—and even more afraid she already had.

Back at the gallery, Camellia dismissed her staff with a single glance. The command needed no words—just the weight of her gaze, cool and unyielding. Eyes averted, they filed out one by one, heads bowed like penitents retreating from a silent judgment. Shoes tapped against marble. A breath was held. The air itself seemed to tighten around her presence. All except one. Vivianne. Her assistant.

"You were on duty when the breach occurred," Camellia said.

"Yes, ma'am. But I never left the hallway. No one went in."

Camellia didn't accuse. She didn't need to. Her presence made every word a lie. Her stillness was louder than fury, her elegance more terrifying than violence. The silence between them stretched razor-thin. Vivianne's knuckles whitened around the folder she clutched, her stance rigid, rehearsed. But fear crept in anyway—slow, suffocating. Not because she had done anything wrong, but because Camellia's scrutiny spared no one, and even innocence could shatter under the intensity of it.

Vivianne had followed every protocol. She knew she had. But knowing didn't lessen the pressure. Being in Camellia's presence was like standing on the edge of a blade—one wrong move and everything would split. Her mind raced through timestamps, camera angles, alibis she didn't need but mentally rehearsed anyway. She wasn't defending herself. She was surviving something far more dangerous: Camellia's attention.

Every second without a reply felt like a blade being sharpened. Vivianne's breath came shorter, her pulse visible at the hollow of her throat. She had seen Camellia dismantle reputations with a whisper, sever careers with a look. And now, she stood in that spotlight—not as a target, but as a witness. And even that felt like standing too close to a fire that chose its fuel at will.

The walls felt too close, the silence too wide. The air smelled faintly of lilies and ozone, like a storm held at bay by will alone. Vivianne swallowed, the sound loud in her own ears. Her answer had been truthful. But truth had never been armor in this place. Not under Camellia's gaze. Her hands didn't shake, but they ached with the effort not to.

She turned to Alex. "If you're going to lie to me, do it well. I don't tolerate cowardice."

Alex, blushing and breathless, nodded. A little too quickly.

His collar was crooked. His lips still bore the faintest mark of Maris's lipstick. His hands twitched like he didn't know what to do with them. The room had become a crucible, and he was melting by degrees. And Camellia, ever composed, ever patient, watched him squirm with the cool amusement of a cat toying with something soft and breakable.

The room felt rigged—each breath a wire, each glance a snare. And in the center, Camellia stood like a beautiful executioner, polished and still. Her gaze was a mirror and a weapon, forcing reflection, inviting collapse.

There was nowhere for him to run. No line rehearsed well enough. No version of the truth that wouldn't cost him something. Every flicker of movement under her gaze felt like a mistake. Her silence was worse than scorn—it was strategy.

Camellia smiled.

The theatre had only just begun.

Chapter Four: A Canvas of Lies

The cool, calculated silence of the gallery pressed in around them, thick and suffocating like the air before a storm. Alex stood near the door, his fingers gripping the edge of the frame, knuckles pale from the pressure. He was rigid, trying to anchor himself against the uncertainty that clawed at him. The aftermath of their encounter still pulsed through him—a mix of desire, guilt, and something darker, something far more dangerous.

The erotic tension they had shared the night before had bled into this moment, but now, it twisted into something sinister. The heat between them had cooled, and in its place, doubt and suspicion loomed like shadows.

Her words echoed in his mind, haunting him: *"I'm not the one you should be afraid of, Alex. Don't forget that."* The threat had been spoken with the same intensity as their passion, but now, it had taken root inside him. Every glance from Camellia felt like a test, every word she spoke felt like a trap.

He couldn't shake the feeling that the reason for the fracture in their dynamic wasn't his failure as a lover—it was something deeper. Something he hadn't seen coming. Something that was now unraveling in front of him.

Camellia's silhouette stood at the center of the gallery, her back to him, framed by the soft, ambient light. She was a vision of control—unmoved, untouchable. But inside, her thoughts spun rapidly, weaving a web of strategy, of manipulation. The night before had been a test. A chance to push Alex, to see just how far she could bend him. But now, standing in the wake of their encounter, she knew something was wrong.

Her surveillance had been disturbed. It had been subtle at first, a small glitch that could have been dismissed. But last night, it had been undeniable.

Someone had breached her carefully crafted defenses. Someone with access.

Her pulse quickened as she pieced it together, and the answer was clear—*it was him.*

She turned slowly, locking her eyes with his as he stood by the door, shifting uncomfortably. He didn't fill the room the way he had the night before. There was a wariness in his posture now, a hesitancy that made her stomach tighten with both excitement and caution.

He's unraveling, she thought. *But I can make him unravel further.*

She stepped forward, her heels clicking against the polished floor, each step deliberate, slow, like a predator closing in on its prey. The tension in the room thickened with each inch she gained.

Her voice broke the silence, smooth and lethal. "One night," she began, her tone deliberately slow, every word dripping with intent. "One night, and yet, I'm left wondering—was that your game, Alex? Or was I simply another part of your strategy?"

Her eyes never left his face, studying every flicker of emotion, every subtle shift in his gaze. His jaw clenched, his breath quickening, betraying the turmoil she had expected. She could see the vulnerability hiding beneath the surface, and that was exactly what she needed.

She closed the distance between them, stepping so close she could feel the heat radiating from his body. The air between them seemed to hum with the tension, thick and suffocating.

"You've always been good at playing both sides, haven't you?" Her voice was cutting, deliberate in its cruelty. "Always bending to whoever holds the power, always pretending to be on their side. But now, I need to know, Alex..." Her lips curled into a smile that was anything but kind. "Did you cause the disturbance in my surveillance last night?"

Her words were like a knife, cutting through the facade he had built. She wasn't just asking—she was accusing, making him feel the weight of his own guilt even if he wasn't fully aware of it yet.

She studied him, watching for any sign of hesitation, of panic, of fear. Every second felt like an eternity. The slightest flicker of movement, the tightening of his chest, the tremor in his fingers—everything was telling her what she already knew.

He was lying.

Alex felt the breath catch in his throat, and for a moment, everything around him went still. Camellia's question—so pointed, so direct—knocked the wind out of him. He had known this moment would come, had braced for it, but now that it was here, he was unprepared.

Her gaze pierced through him like a laser, cold and unforgiving. The room felt smaller with each passing second, her presence overwhelming him, suffocating him. The very air between them had turned to stone.

His heart raced. He could lie. He could say anything. But something in her eyes, something in the way she stood there, made him hesitate.

She knows. The thought hit him like a blow. She knew, and he couldn't escape it.

"I didn't—" His voice cracked, and he hated how weak it sounded. The lie caught in his throat.

"You didn't?" Camellia's voice was a whisper, cutting through his defense like a blade. "You didn't cause the disturbance? Or you didn't mean to? You think I believe that?"

She stepped closer, closing the gap between them, and in that moment, the distance between their bodies felt like an ocean. Her gaze never wavered, drilling into him, pushing him further into a corner with every breath.

"I hope you're not lying to me, Alex," she said softly, her voice a velvet caress that was laced with venom. "Because I will find out. And if you are the one who's been watching me..." She let the words hang in the air like a promise. "I'll make sure you regret it."

Her smile widened, but her eyes remained cold. The softness of her voice belied the danger that lurked beneath the surface. She wasn't just toying with him anymore. She was taking control. She was taking everything from him.

And with each word, each movement, she was stripping away his defenses, layer by layer. The power was hers now.

She could feel him breaking. His breath was shallow now, uneven. His shoulders were tight with the weight of his guilt, but it wasn't the guilt of what he had done—it was the guilt of being caught. She could see the doubt in his eyes, the flicker of uncertainty, and that was all she needed to tighten her grip on him even more.

She leaned in, her voice dropping even lower, the words slipping like honey from her lips. "You know, Alex," she purred, "I think you might be starting to believe your own lies."

She allowed the words to linger in the air, watching him squirm, watching him try to hold on to whatever semblance of control he had left. She could feel the confusion, the self-doubt swirling inside him, and she knew she had him exactly where she wanted him.

It's not just about the surveillance. She could see it in him now—the way he shifted, the way he couldn't look her in the eye. She was no longer just testing him—she was breaking him.

"You'll regret playing this game with me, Alex," she whispered, her smile widening, her fingers brushing lightly against his arm in a mock gesture of tenderness. "I always win."

She stepped back, letting the silence fill the room once more. This was just the beginning. The game was no longer about who held power—it was about who would break first. And Camellia was going to make sure it wasn't her.

The silence between them stretched, thick and suffocating, as Camellia stood before him. Alex's chest rose and fell unevenly, his mind a storm of confusion and guilt, but he couldn't bring himself to speak. He wanted to say something—anything—that would shift the tension, that would free him from the invisible trap she had set. But the words wouldn't come.

Camellia's presence was like a weight bearing down on him, every breath he took feeling heavier than the last. She hadn't broken eye contact, her cold gaze never leaving his face, and that was the part that unsettled him the most. She wasn't just playing with him—she was dissecting him, exposing his every weakness.

For a moment, he wondered if she even needed him to answer her question, or if the truth had already been revealed in the way he trembled before her. *Had he betrayed her?* He couldn't even tell anymore. His mind was tangled in lies, and the longer she held him in her gaze, the more he found himself questioning everything he had believed about their connection.

But he couldn't escape her. Not now. Not ever.

Camellia tilted her head slightly, observing him, her smile curling ever so slightly at the edges. It was the kind of smile that didn't belong to someone who had just been betrayed, and yet, there it was—mischief, amusement, and something darker, a quiet triumph in her eyes.

"Tell me, Alex," she purred, her voice soft and sweet as a blade, "how long do you think you can keep up this charade?"

Her words were poison-coated honey, and they wrapped around him like chains. The more he fought to breathe, the tighter they became.

She took a step back, allowing the space between them to grow again, but her presence still lingered, heavy in the air. The power dynamic had shifted so violently, so completely, that Alex no longer knew where he stood.

Camellia moved slowly, casually, toward the center of the gallery. Her heels clicked against the floor in a rhythmic pattern that seemed to echo in the room like the ticking of a clock. Time, it seemed, was her weapon, and she was wielding it expertly.

"You think you've got me figured out," she said, her voice low, almost conversational, but there was a sharp edge that cut through every word. "You think you understand this game we're playing. But you're just a pawn, Alex."

Her eyes narrowed, as if assessing him for the final strike. "You always were. You just didn't realize it yet."

Alex's heart pounded in his chest, a wild rhythm that threatened to betray him. He had always prided himself on being able to navigate between the lines, on seeing through the masks people wore. But Camellia... Camellia was different. She didn't wear a mask. She was the mask. And every time he thought he saw the truth, she showed him another layer, another hidden face beneath the one he had come to know.

"You're not as clever as you think," she continued, her tone mocking now, as if she were speaking to a child who had just realized it was in over its head. "You thought you could control me, manipulate me into believing you were the answer. But you're not. You're just another distraction in my path."

Her words were like daggers, each one striking a new wound. He wanted to lash out, to defend himself, but the words caught in his throat. What could he say? What could he do when she was this far ahead of him, when she held all the cards?

She paused, her back turned to him, and for a moment, the silence seemed to stretch into eternity. Then, without turning around, she spoke again, her voice cutting through the quiet like a whip.

"But that's the thing about games, Alex," she said, her tone darkening. "Eventually, the pieces fall where they're meant to."

Alex swallowed hard, the knot in his throat making it feel impossible to breathe. The weight of her words pressed down on him, suffocating him with their truth. He was a fool. He had known it for some time, but hearing her say it aloud made the reality of it settle like ice in his veins.

Every part of him screamed to fight back, to claw his way out of this web she had woven around him, but he couldn't. He was trapped, caught in the very game he had thought he was controlling.

"You've won, Camellia," he said, his voice strained, the words slipping out before he could stop them. "What more do you want from me?"

She finally turned to face him, and the look in her eyes sent a chill down his spine. There was no sympathy, no mercy. Just cold, calculating power. The predator and the prey, caught in an eternal dance.

"More?" She smiled, a flash of something dark in her gaze. "I want you to break, Alex. I want you to understand just how much control you've lost. I want you to understand that there's nothing you can do to change this. You will never be the one in charge."

Her voice softened, almost sweet, but it only made the words that followed sting harder.

"You thought you could win me over," she murmured, stepping closer to him again, her breath warm against his skin. "But you never stood a chance."

Alex's heart was pounding in his chest. Every instinct told him to run, to escape, but the truth was worse than any lie he could have spun. He had no escape. No way out.

Camellia's eyes lingered on Alex, drinking in the helplessness she saw reflected there. This was the moment she had been waiting for—the moment where she could finally make him feel the weight of his own vulnerability. It wasn't just about him confessing his guilt—it was about breaking him, about making him realize how insignificant he truly was in her world.

She reached out slowly, a deliberate movement, her fingers trailing along his jaw, the touch light, almost tender. But it was anything but gentle. It was a reminder of who controlled the game.

"Remember this moment, Alex," she whispered, her breath soft against his ear. "This is the beginning of the end for you. And once I've broken you, there will be no going back."

With a final glance, she withdrew, leaving him standing in the center of the room, his breath ragged, his body tense, caught in the snare she had so carefully set. She didn't need to say anything else. The truth was in the air, in the way he looked at her, in the way he knew he had already lost.

The game was over. She had won.

Camellia moved through the gallery with a deliberate grace, her heels clicking against the marble floor, each step echoing in the empty space like a countdown. The tension in the room had been suffocating, but she had found satisfaction in it—Alex was broken, and she could feel the heat of victory seeping through her veins. But there was still more to be done.

She needed to regroup, to reassert her control in the quiet comfort of her sanctuary. She had already toyed with Alex, forced him to see just how powerless he was in her presence, but there were still pieces to be placed. The game was far from over.

She stepped into her office, the cool, minimalist design of the space offering a sharp contrast to the emotional chaos that had unfolded moments before. Her breath was even, measured, as she moved to the window, looking out over the Seine.

The night had already begun to fall, casting a soft, golden hue over the water, but Camellia felt none of the serenity the view might have inspired. The only thing that lingered in her mind was the taste of control, and the promise of what was still to come.

Vivianne entered the room quietly, as always, her footsteps light against the polished floors. She knew Camellia well enough to sense the change in the air—the tension that had followed her boss into the room, that barely contained energy that radiated from her. It wasn't just from the encounter with Alex, though Vivianne was sure that had been part of it. No, this was something deeper, something only Camellia truly understood.

Her eyes softened as she took in Camellia's posture, the way she stood by the window, gazing out at the city as if it were her domain. Vivianne had worked with Camellia for years, and over time, she had learned the nuances of her moods, the shifts that few others would notice. She could see that Camellia wasn't just calculating her next move—she was *weighing* it. There was something darker, something more dangerous in the air tonight.

"How did it go?" Vivianne's voice was soft, almost an afterthought, but there was an edge of concern buried beneath her cool tone. She had learned early on not to push too hard, but tonight, she could sense the shift in the energy, and she didn't want to be left in the dark.

Camellia didn't immediately respond, her back still to Vivianne, her fingers lightly tracing the edge of the glass. The silence stretched between them, and Vivianne's patience began to fray, wondering if she would have to ask again.

She let the silence settle before turning around, her gaze sharp, but unreadable. Her lips curled into a smile, one that was more controlled, more calculated than the one she had given Alex. "It went exactly as I planned," she said, her voice smooth, almost too calm.

She moved toward the desk, fingers brushing lightly against the edges of the papers strewn across it—deliberate, as if considering her next step.

"But Alex," she continued, her smile faltering just slightly, "isn't nearly as clever as he thinks. He's already unraveling. I've given him just enough to question everything."

Vivianne watched her carefully, her brow furrowing in silent concern. There was something in Camellia's demeanor that unsettled her—a darkness that had only grown more pronounced in recent months. Vivianne had always been loyal to Camellia, but there was a quiet part of her that sometimes wondered how much of herself was left in the woman she served. How much of that control was truly her own?

"Are you sure you're not pushing him too far?" Vivianne asked, her voice quieter now, a trace of worry slipping through her usual coolness. "You don't

44

need him broken. You need him useful."

Camellia paused, her eyes locking with Vivianne's, and for the briefest moment, there was a flicker of something deeper—something that felt almost vulnerable. But just as quickly, the mask slipped back into place.

"Useful?" Camellia echoed, her voice low and cutting. "No, Vivianne. What I need is to remind him that he has no control. When someone is broken, when they're forced to face their own helplessness, they'll do anything to regain that power. And in that desperation, they become more useful than they could ever be before."

She leaned back against the desk, her gaze turning inward for a moment. "I won't stop until Alex realizes that. Not until he understands exactly who holds the reins."

Vivianne nodded, but there was a faint unease that still lingered in her chest. She had seen Camellia manipulate others, break them down, rebuild them into whatever image suited her. But she had never seen her quite like this. There was an intensity now, a coldness that made Vivianne wonder if even Camellia knew where this path would lead.

"Is that all?" Vivianne asked, though it was more of a statement than a question. She was already anticipating the next set of orders, the next move to be made.

"Not yet," Camellia replied, her tone suddenly sharp. "I still have to deal with the other piece of this puzzle. But for now, I need you to handle the next phase."

Vivianne nodded, stepping closer, her gaze not leaving Camellia's as she spoke. "Of course. What do you need?"

Camellia gave her a long, considering look. "I need you to handle our next move—find out where Alex's loyalties really lie. I need to know everything, Vivianne. Everything he's hiding. And I need it quickly."

There was a pause before Camellia's lips curled again, a flicker of something dangerously amused in her eyes. "If Alex thinks this game is over, he has another thing coming."

Camellia remained seated at the edge of the desk, her fingers lightly tapping the surface, as if contemplating something beyond the words she had already spoken. Vivianne stood across from her, waiting for the next shift, the next layer of the game to unfold. Camellia's silence was deliberate, and Vivianne knew better than to rush her.

The stillness between them hung heavy, filled with the unspoken tension that only existed between those who truly understood each other.

"You're not telling me everything," Vivianne said softly, her gaze steady. There was no accusation in her voice—just an acknowledgment. She had learned long ago that Camellia never shared her full hand until it was absolutely necessary. But this... this felt different. Vivianne could sense the undercurrent of doubt, of something slipping beneath the surface that even Camellia wasn't fully in control of.

Camellia's eyes flickered toward her, sharp, cutting. Her lips parted just slightly, then curled into a smile—one that didn't reach her eyes.

"Of course, I'm not." She leaned forward, her voice lowering, softer now. "But you're right. There's more, Vivianne. More than I let on." She paused, her gaze drifting toward the window, her thoughts seemingly far away. The gallery, the people, the games—it was all part of the puzzle, but something had shifted.

She turned back to Vivianne, her eyes intense, searching, as though weighing something that might not yet be fully formed in her mind.

"I think there's another player involved in all of this. Someone else has been manipulating the pieces," Camellia admitted, her tone careful, deliberate.

Vivianne's brow furrowed slightly, confusion passing briefly across her face. "Another player? You think someone's behind the breach?"

"Not just the breach," Camellia replied, her voice quiet with growing certainty. "The disruption at the gallery... the one with the man that caused a scene. It wasn't just random, Vivianne. It felt too precise, too deliberate. It was a warning. A test." She leaned forward again, her gaze never leaving Vivianne's. "Someone knew exactly how to disrupt the systems without triggering the alarms. Someone who thought they understood the vulnerabilities I've worked so hard to keep hidden still made a mistake. And that's not just a coincidence."

Vivianne absorbed her words carefully, her mind whirring as she processed the information. "You think it was someone within the gallery? Another employee? Or something more... external?"

"I don't know yet," Camellia replied, her voice calm but laced with tension. "But I *do* know it's someone who understands the stakes. Someone who might be watching, waiting for the right moment to make their move. The systems are secure, Vivianne. I've made sure of that. But whoever this is, they've found a way in. And now, they're playing their own game."

Vivianne's expression hardened, her sharp mind already piecing together the fragments. "If someone is playing us, then we need to find them before they make their next move. How are you going to handle this, Camellia?"

Camellia's eyes glinted, a flicker of her usual confidence returning. "I'll handle it the way I always do. I'll find them, Vivianne. And when I do, they'll regret ever thinking they could challenge me."

There was a long pause before Camellia spoke again, her voice almost a whisper, as though she were revealing a deeper, more personal truth. "But I can't move too quickly, Vivianne. I need to bait them, pull them closer, and make them believe they're in control. That's how this works. They don't know I'm already watching them. And I'll wait until the perfect moment to strike."

Vivianne's lips pressed together in contemplation. She had seen this side of Camellia before—the careful strategist, the patient manipulator who could weave a plan months in advance. But there was something about this situation that felt different. This wasn't just about power or control. It felt personal. And that made Vivianne uneasy.

"What if this person has already gotten too close?" Vivianne asked carefully, a note of concern slipping into her voice. "What if they're already working within your inner circle?"

Camellia's eyes narrowed slightly, the edge of a threat lingering in her gaze. "If they're close, Vivianne, they'll reveal themselves soon enough. But I will not be outplayed. Not by anyone."

She stood up abruptly, her movements fluid, as if the conversation had shifted into the realm of action. The air seemed to hum with her resolve.

"I trust you to handle things on your end," Camellia continued, her tone back to its usual level of command. "Keep Alex in line for now. Don't let him slip away. And make sure the gallery stays under tight surveillance. I want to know the moment someone steps out of line. We can't afford to overlook any details."

Vivianne nodded, but there was a flicker of something in her eyes—a lingering uncertainty, a question that hadn't been answered. She had followed Camellia loyally for years, but this… this felt like something darker, something she wasn't sure she could follow without question.

As she turned to leave, Vivianne hesitated for a moment, then spoke again, her voice lower, almost too quiet.

"And if this person is closer than we think?" she asked, her words heavy with implication.

Camellia paused, her back still to Vivianne. She didn't turn around, but her voice was ice-cold when she spoke.

"Then we'll have to make them think they're in control," Camellia replied softly. "And when they're ready to reveal themselves, we'll be waiting. They won't know what hit them."

Vivianne was leaving the room, but her thoughts stayed with Camellia's words. The tension in the air, the urgency, the certainty that Camellia would find a way to destroy anyone who dared challenge her—it was all too familiar. But the shadow of doubt still lingered in the back of her mind. Who was this new player? And more importantly—what would happen if they were already too deeply embedded in Camellia's world to root out?

Vivianne hesitated at the door, her hand resting on the cool handle, but Camellia's voice stopped her before she could leave.

"Vivianne," Camellia called, her tone darker now, tinged with something dangerous. She turned, her eyes focused, narrowing as she fixed her gaze on her assistant.

Vivianne turned back slowly, catching the shift in Camellia's demeanor. There was a flicker of something unreadable in her eyes, a calculation that hinted at a deeper layer of this unfolding drama.

"I think I know who's behind this," Camellia continued, her voice low, almost a growl. "And I don't think they're working alone."

Vivianne frowned, her brow furrowing as she stepped back into the room. "You have someone specific in mind?"

Camellia's lips curled into a thin, knowing smile. She moved closer to Vivianne, her expression hardening as she spoke. "I have my suspicions, yes. You know who controls the market around here, Vivianne. Who has the resources to cause this kind of disruption."

Vivianne's thoughts immediately snapped to Jules Devereux, the wealthy businessman who had made waves in the art world recently. He had always been a thorn in Camellia's side, an opportunist with a mind for acquisitions. But until now, he had never posed a serious threat.

Camellia's smile grew colder. "I think Devereux is involved. He's been eyeing the gallery for months now. It wouldn't surprise me if he's been looking for a way to undercut me, to destabilize my control."

Vivianne's lips pressed together, her mind racing. "You think he's responsible for the breach? That he's been using your own systems against you?"

"Not directly," Camellia replied, her voice deliberate, almost casual as if this were just another move in a long chess game. "But I do think he's the one pulling the strings. He's done this before, Vivianne. A man like Devereux doesn't just want power—he wants to control it all. If I were him, I'd use every tool at my disposal to make sure my rivals fell. The gallery, my reputation... this isn't just about art. It's about the people who own it."

Her gaze flickered towards the window again, her eyes narrowing. "And Devereux is the one who thinks he can take it from me."

Vivianne's face hardened as she digested this new piece of information. Jules Devereux wasn't just a businessman—he was a player in the shadows, a man known for manipulating his way to the top by exploiting every weakness he could find. If Camellia was right, then the stakes had just been raised significantly.

"How are you going to handle him?" Vivianne asked, her voice steady, though she could hear the edge of concern creeping in. She knew that Devereux was no ordinary adversary, and his involvement would complicate things.

Camellia's smile never wavered. "I'll bait him, of course. I'll make him think he has the upper hand, and when he's close enough, I'll show him how wrong he is. The only thing Devereux understands is power, and I'm more than capable of showing him just how much control I truly have."

She paused, her eyes glinting with a predatory gleam. "But first, I need to see what kind of moves he makes. What he *thinks* he knows. And once he believes he's in the driver's seat, that's when I'll strike."

Vivianne nodded, a slight shiver running down her spine at the thought of what Camellia had in store. This wasn't just a game of business—it was personal now. And if Devereux had underestimated Camellia, he would soon learn the hard way that she was not a woman to be toyed with.

"Understood," Vivianne said, her voice firm now. "I'll get started on monitoring him. We need to stay one step ahead."

Camellia straightened, her posture regal, a leader preparing for war. "Keep your eyes open. If Devereux is behind this, he'll reveal himself soon enough. And when he does, we'll be waiting."

She turned away, her back now to Vivianne, as if the conversation were already over. "And, Vivianne," she added over her shoulder, her voice low and filled with a chilling confidence, "make sure you stay close. This game is about to get a lot more complicated, and I'll need all the pieces in place before I make my next move."

As Vivianne exited the room, she could feel the weight of Camellia's words pressing on her shoulders. The revelation about Devereux shifted everything. This wasn't just a business rivalry anymore—it was a battle for control, a war being fought in the shadows.

Vivianne's thoughts turned over the last few months, recalling the quiet whispers that had circulated about Devereux's ambitions. It had always seemed like idle chatter, but now, everything clicked into place. The disruption at the gallery—the breach in the systems—the mounting pressure on Camellia's empire—it all pointed to Devereux's calculated moves.

She could sense that this was more than just a professional threat; this was personal. Camellia didn't just want to win. She wanted to destroy anyone who thought they could take what was hers.

Chapter Five: Soft Chains, Silent Mouths

Camellia watched Vivianne leave the office, her heels clicking sharply against the polished floor as she walked down the corridor, her footsteps firm and purposeful. The tension from earlier in the evening had already begun to fade into a distant memory, replaced by the unshakable sense of control that had always defined Camellia's every move. She was alone now, but it didn't matter. The moment was hers to claim.

With Vivianne dispatched to handle Devereux, the pieces of her plan were already in motion. Camellia didn't need to rush. All she had to do now was wait. The thought filled her with a thrill, a kind of satisfaction she hadn't felt in a long time. The game was shifting in her favor, and this time, no one—no one—would be able to stop her. Not Alex, not Devereux, not a single soul.

Her fingers lightly traced the edge of the desk, the smooth surface grounding her in the quiet calm that had enveloped the room. The anticipation was almost palpable. She allowed herself a brief smile, savoring the stillness before the inevitable storm of events that would soon follow.

Just as she reached for her coat, her phone buzzed softly on the desk, breaking the silence. Camellia glanced down, her eyes narrowing slightly as she saw the name on the screen—Maris.

A smile flickered on her lips, though it was colder now, sharper—marked with a faint bitterness that only someone like Camellia could hold. Maris. Her muse. Her creation. A beautiful, unpredictable thing that she had shaped and held close, only for it to slip through her fingers when she needed her most.

The memory of Japan—the look on Maris's face when she walked out, leaving Camellia standing in the ruins of their connection—still lingered, a jagged edge of pride and betrayal that cut deeper than Camellia would ever admit. They had danced a dangerous waltz, intertwining bodies and minds in a blur of passion and dominance, control and submission. The dynamics had always played out exactly as Camellia intended—until that night.

Now, Maris's absence was a mere blip—faint, fleeting, and easily ignored. The way she hesitated in their calls, the subtle resistance in her voice, it grated against Camellia, stirring a raw, familiar hurt. It had been one year since that night in Japan—the night full of fire and raw need, the night that had bound them so completely. The night Maris had left without a word, walking away from everything they had shared. Camellia had felt the sting of it, the hollow ache of Maris's absence, and yet, it wasn't something she allowed herself to dwell on. *She would return.*

This was the first time they had come into contact since then, and at the time Camellia had eventually convinced herself the distance would be temporary. Maris had left her once, but now, she knew it wasn't permanent. Maris might pull away, might try to resist, but Camellia understood the pull—the hunger Maris had for what only Camellia could give her. It was inevitable. It always was. The craving, the need, would always draw her back. No matter how far she tried to run, no matter how much she resisted.

The truth was clear, even if Maris didn't yet know it: after the night in the mirrored room, she would return. It was just a matter of time.

Camellia answered the call without a moment's hesitation, her voice smooth and unbothered, a practiced mask of calm. It was the same tone she always used when she held someone's world in the palm of her hand. She had all the power, and she knew it.

"Maris," Camellia purred, her voice light but laced with something far more dangerous, a quiet possessiveness that Maris couldn't escape. "What's on your mind?"

A brief silence lingered on the other end of the line, the hesitation in Maris's voice almost palpable. Camellia could feel the tension, the resistance that Maris always tried to hide. It was the kind of fragile defiance Maris had never been able to sustain for long. This wasn't the first time she'd pulled away, and it wouldn't be the last. But each time, it only made the inevitable return all the sweeter.

"I didn't expect you to answer the call," Maris said, her voice betraying a hint of uncertainty before she quickly reined it in. "I've been busy. Just thinking about things."

Camellia's lips curled into a soft smile, though there was nothing soft in her voice when she responded. "Thinking about things?" she mused, her tone cool but edged with command. "Or thinking about me?"

Maris's grip tightened on the phone, her fingers trembling slightly, but she didn't let it show. "I—" she began, but the words faltered before she could finish.

"Don't think you can just run from me, Maris," Camellia continued, her voice now softer, more coaxing, but still laced with steel. "You can pull away all you like, but we both know you will come back. You need me. Want me."

The words hung in the air between them, heavy with meaning. Maris, in her fragile resistance, didn't yet realize how tightly Camellia had woven the web around her. No matter how far she tried to escape, she would always come back. She always did.

"I didn't call you for this," Maris said, trying to push back, but even as she spoke, she knew her words carried no weight. The history between them was undeniable, and Camellia's power over her was just as real as ever.

Camellia's voice softened, almost like a whisper. "It's funny, Maris. You say you didn't call for this, but here you are. We both know the truth, don't we? You're mine. You always have been."

A shiver ran down Maris's spine, the way Camellia spoke sending a rush of conflicting emotions through her. She wanted to fight it. To push it all away. But the truth was—Camellia was right. Maris had never truly escaped her.

"I'm not the same person I was when I left," Maris replied, her voice low and steady, but she could feel the crack in it, the hesitation.

Camellia's laughter rang softly in her ear, warm and knowing. "No, Maris. You're not. But you'll never be free of me. You *want* this. You want me, just like you always have."

The words clung to her like a weight, and Maris closed her eyes for a brief moment, trying to steady herself. The pull was too strong. She could feel it, as if Camellia's words were a chain, soft and silent, wrapping around her heart.

"I'll be waiting for you," Camellia said, her voice honey-sweet but sharp, as if this were nothing more than a game. "You always come back, Maris. You always do."

She could hear the shift in Camellia's tone, that cold edge returning. "I know exactly what you're thinking," Camellia purred, her voice velvet but sharp. "But you'll come back to me, just like you always do. You need me, Maris. You want me."

Maris clenched her jaw, the familiar ache of Camellia's words biting deeper than she wanted to admit. *She always said that. Always made me believe it.*

But she knew that wasn't the whole truth.

"Camellia, I—" Maris began but was cut off by the sound of someone approaching from behind. The pulse of urgency in her veins quickened, not from the conversation with Camellia, but because she had a different task to attend to.

Before she could process the shift in her thoughts, the voice of her cousin Kenji rang out from the street ahead. "Maris."

Her heart skipped, and she quickly ended the call with Camellia. The line went dead, leaving her to face the reality of her other life—the one Camellia could never know about.

Kenji stood with his arms crossed in the shadow of an old, ivy-clad building, watching Maris as she ended her call and approached. Despite their shared background, he knew better than anyone that their roles in the underground world required discretion. This was business, and business didn't care for personal connections.

"Had to cut it short?" Kenji asked, raising an eyebrow as Maris joined him on the corner.

She nodded, her face flickering with a touch of frustration before she concealed it behind a practiced smile. "I didn't have much choice. She's persistent."

Kenji's gaze softened, but only for a moment. "She always has been." His voice lowered. "But it's not her you need to worry about right now, is it?"

Maris sighed deeply, her gaze shifting down the street as if expecting someone else to appear. She shook her head, the weight of her dual life pressing on her chest like a heavy fog. "No. I've got another job. Can't stay too long. It's the usual setup—nothing you need to worry about."

Kenji gave her a look that didn't need words. They had both been raised in this world of shadows, and neither of them had ever really left it. He knew the real reason she had come back into Camellia's orbit. She was playing her role, but the task she'd taken on was always in the back of her mind, a constant reminder that her loyalty to Camellia was... *temporary*.

Maris hesitated, glancing at him. "You heard about the surveillance breach?"

Kenji's lips curled into a subtle smile. "I've heard whispers, but nothing solid. You working on that, too?"

She didn't answer immediately. She only offered a faint nod, her eyes clouding with a mix of determination and reluctance. "Just don't let it interfere with your job, Kenji. We've got rules for a reason."

Kenji chuckled, the sound dry and knowing. "I respect customer privacy. You should know that by now."

Maris gave him a tight smile, but her mind was elsewhere. The job she had been given wasn't just about keeping an eye on Camellia or Devereux. It was about something bigger—an opportunity to prove herself in a world that had always been just a little too far out of reach.

It was a world she knew too well. And now, more than ever, it was calling her name.

The cool night air brushed against Maris's skin as she walked briskly down the street, her mind still buzzing with the remnants of her call with Camellia. She had always known the way Camellia worked, how she could turn even the simplest words into weapons of control. And yet, as much as Maris wanted to fight against it, there was still something about Camellia's hold on her that was impossible to ignore.

But now, that wasn't her reality. Not anymore. Tonight, she had a different mission—a mission she could never share with Camellia. She had been playing her part in the shadows for too long, and this was her chance to take control of her own fate. Her cousin, Kenji, was the only one who understood the weight of what she was doing, and his quiet presence beside her reminded her that she wasn't alone in this.

They walked in silence, their footsteps synchronized in the cool evening air. Kenji's watchful eyes scanned their surroundings, always alert. Even in a city as vast and anonymous as Paris, there were still eyes that could betray you. Maris felt the familiar weight of her dual life press on her shoulders.

This job, this secret mission she had taken on, wasn't about money, nor was it about power—it was about control. The control she had always craved but never truly held, the control she was determined to claim for herself.

Kenji's low voice broke the silence. "I know this feels like a game," he said, his tone calm but with an undercurrent of something deeper. "But remember— the stakes are high. Don't let your emotions cloud your judgment. You know how easily that can happen."

Maris stiffened slightly but kept her eyes forward, focusing on the path ahead. "I know," she replied firmly, her voice steady. "But this is different. This time, it's not just about being the perfect shadow. I'm done being anyone's puppet."

Kenji gave her a knowing look, though he didn't press further. He had seen this side of Maris before—had seen her grow from a willing participant in the games of others to someone desperate to carve out her own path. But he also knew the cost of that kind of change. It was never as simple as walking away. There would be consequences, and Maris wasn't fully ready for them.

They continued walking, the hum of the city surrounding them. Maris's thoughts kept returning to her mission. It wasn't just about surveillance or gathering information. This was her chance to prove herself—her chance to move beyond the walls Camellia had built around her, beyond the pull of their handler's dangerous world. She wasn't the same person who had been swept up in those worlds before. No, now she was someone else. Someone who could finally choose her own direction.

As they turned a corner, Kenji's pace slowed, and he looked at her intently. "Don't get lost in the game, Maris. It's easy to forget what you're really fighting for."

She stopped and met his gaze, her eyes hardening with resolve. "I'm not lost, Kenji. I'm exactly where I need to be."

His lips twitched into a brief smile, and for a moment, he didn't look like the quiet, calculating man she had known all her life. Instead, there was a flicker of something else—understanding, maybe even a little worry. "Just be careful. This world isn't kind to those who think they can control it. It has a way of breaking them."

Maris swallowed the lump in her throat. She had heard the warning before, and though it had always lingered in her mind, tonight it felt heavier. But this was her choice. She was taking control, and she wouldn't back down.

"I will," she said quietly, but her voice was laced with determination. "I'm ready."

Kenji nodded and patted her shoulder briefly, then stepped back into the shadows, disappearing into the city's endless web. Maris stood still for a moment, letting the weight of his words settle. She could feel the pressure of what lay ahead—her mission, her future, and the inescapable pull of the life she had left behind.

She had a chance now. A chance to prove she could break free. Whether that would set her free or trap her further, only time would tell.

But for now, she walked forward into the unknown, her heart steady and her mind clear. Whatever happened next, it was her move.

As the evening stretched on, Camellia stood by the window of her office, watching the city breathe beneath her—an endless sea of lights that flickered in sync with the pulse of her thoughts. The night had settled into a rhythm, quiet but charged, much like the calm before the storm she had prepared for. Her fingers idly traced the glass, each movement deliberate, as if plotting the trajectory of her life, her power, in the very fabric of the world that lay just beyond her reach.

The gallery had been quieter than usual over the past few days. Not that she minded. Silence was something she controlled, something that worked to her advantage. The absence of noise allowed her the space to think, to observe, to wait. But the stillness was temporary.

The next showing was already on the horizon—a carefully orchestrated event that had been in the making for weeks. A new collection, a fresh wave of art to invigorate the gallery's elite patrons and reinstate her dominance in the cultural undercurrent. As always, there would be whispers—whispers of power, of influence, of the dark alliances forged under the roof of Galerie Solé.

Tonight, however, Camellia wasn't entirely focused on the show. There was still a lingering sense of unfinished business—Maris's resistance, Devereux's scheming, and Alex's increasing uncertainty. But, as she always did, she pushed those thoughts aside, refocusing on the task at hand. The art. The game.

The gallery was alive with movement as the morning sun began to cast its pale light over the polished floors. Staff moved quickly, preparing for the evening's showing. The walls, adorned with newly hung pieces, gleamed with anticipation, as if each brushstroke contained its own hidden meaning, waiting for the right eyes to decipher it.

Camellia watched the preparations from the balcony of her office, taking in the subtle shifts in the space. Every detail, every angle mattered. She ran her fingers through her hair, a soft, almost imperceptible gesture of control. The artists she worked with—some she had chosen carefully, others by sheer circumstance—had provided her with a new collection that would cement her position. And for tonight, the world would be watching.

Her gaze moved down to the bustling floor below, where Vivianne was coordinating the final touches. Her loyal assistant. Camellia had always known the value of a well-oiled machine, and Vivianne had long been an integral part of hers.

But even Vivianne couldn't escape the tension that hung in the air. It was there, thick and waiting, like a storm that hadn't yet broken.

The evening crept closer, and the guests began to arrive, their luxury cars lining the street outside the gallery. High heels clicked on the marble floors, voices rose in hushed excitement. The air was electric, charged with the unspoken expectations of those who walked in the circles Camellia had cultivated.

Camellia stood at the entrance, her gaze scanning the crowd, but her mind was elsewhere. She could feel the delicate pressure of her plans shifting with every passing moment. Tonight wasn't just about the art—it was about power. It always was.

Vivianne approached her with a soft smile, handing her a glass of champagne. "Everything's running smoothly, Camellia. The guests are eager. We're ready when you are."

Camellia nodded, accepting the glass, though her eyes remained fixed on the crowd. "Good," she said, her voice as cool as the champagne in her hand. "Make sure the details are handled. No mistakes tonight."

Vivianne bowed her head, stepping away to attend to another matter. As she moved through the crowd, Camellia allowed herself a moment of quiet reflection. Tonight was a reminder—a reminder that no one could truly threaten her position. Not Devereux, not Maris, and certainly not Alex.

Tonight, the gallery would shine once more, and she would remain its brightest star.

The lights dimmed slowly, and the room fell into a collective hush. The air thickened with anticipation, each breath drawn by the guests as they shifted in quiet excitement. Their eyes roamed across the walls, tracing the newly hung collection that Camellia had painstakingly curated. Each piece, a masterstroke of modern artistry, was designed to provoke thought, challenge perceptions, and captivate even the most jaded of critics. She had ensured nothing less.

But it wasn't just the art that would draw them in—it was the experience she had created, the world she had built. The gallery was more than a space for art—it was a sanctuary, a place where control reigned and every moment was calculated. The shadows hung like a veil around the polished, pristine surfaces. A subtle yet undeniable aura of power surrounded her, one that drew her guests deeper into the web she had woven. Tonight, they wouldn't just admire the art—they would *feel* it, breathe it, be enveloped in it.

Whispers of admiration fluttered through the crowd like the gentle rustle of leaves in a breeze. Guests meandered through the space, pausing in front of various pieces—each drawing them in with its depth, its intensity. The first patron who stepped forward to examine a painting—a bold piece full of dark, jagged lines and muted, stormy colors—was mesmerized, his eyes fixed on the complex layers of emotion embedded within the strokes. It was the perfect representation of the subtle power struggles that played out behind the gallery's pristine walls, the perfect juxtaposition of beauty and danger. Camellia knew this was just the beginning—her guests had been drawn in, but now, the real game was about to unfold.

As the evening unfurled, she moved seamlessly through the crowd, a quiet force, unnoticed but felt by everyone in the room. Her presence was undeniable, like an invisible thread that tugged at the very air. Her eyes flickered over the guests, noting their reactions, their gestures—everything mattered. The way they admired the art, the way they whispered in hushed tones to each other, the flicker of desire or confusion in their eyes. Every interaction was a part of the dance she was orchestrating. Camellia knew it was her night to shape, and she reveled in the power of it.

She allowed herself to pause for just a moment in front of one of the paintings. A piece she had commissioned from an artist known for their controversial work—a portrait that seemed to shift and change when you looked at it for too long. The work was provocative, subtle in its layers of emotion, but more importantly, it was *hers*. As her guests moved closer to admire it, she knew they could never truly grasp its meaning, not without understanding the depths of the mind behind it.

But her attention was suddenly pulled away, not by the art, but by the presence of a familiar face. Amid the sea of unknown guests, one person stood out. **Alex.**

He was stationed at the far end of the gallery, leaning slightly against one of the pillars near the entrance, surveying the room with a calm, detached gaze. His posture was stiff, but he held himself well, like the reliable staff member he had been hired to be. His role here was clear—he was a part of the gallery's staff, meant to monitor and assist as needed, and he did so with practiced professionalism. There was no indication of anything out of place, no signs of distraction or hesitation. Camellia had set him in place as a piece of her own larger puzzle, knowing exactly where he would be and what role he would play.

A faint unease stirred in her chest, but Camellia quickly smothered it. *There was nothing to be concerned about.* He was merely doing his job—he always did. He posed no threat. Not to her. Not tonight. But she couldn't help the lingering curiosity in her that brushed against the edges of her mind like a shadow.

Her eyes lingered on him for a moment longer than was necessary, her gaze cool and calculating. *Alex was not a threat.* He was a tool—nothing more.

And yet, the pull of his presence lingered.

She quickly dismissed the thought and turned her attention back to the guests, but not before she caught a flicker of movement—a glance between Alex and one of the patrons. It was subtle, almost imperceptible, but it was there. Her eyes narrowed, studying the interaction. It didn't appear to be anything more than a simple exchange of pleasantries, but something in the way they held each other's gaze made her pause.

Her grip on the edge of her glass tightened, and she immediately turned her focus elsewhere. *Focus on the show,* she reminded herself. The pieces were all falling into place, the night was still young, and everything was proceeding according to her design. No distractions, no uncertainties.

She moved through the crowd again, slipping effortlessly between conversations and whispered admirations, her eyes always keenly watching for the slightest signs of interest or discomfort. She was a presence in the room, unnoticed by many but felt by all. Her guests were here to experience art, to buy art, but the real masterpiece on display tonight was *her.*

And as the evening deepened, she knew—no one would leave the gallery unchanged. Not tonight. Not when she had all the pieces at her fingertips.

The night hummed with the quiet elegance of Galerie Solé, the air thick with the scent of expensive perfumes and the soft clinking of glasses. Alex stood near the back of the gallery, blending into the shadows as he was meant to. His role was simple—monitor the guests, keep an eye on any potential disruptions, and ensure that the flow of the evening remained smooth. He had done this countless times before, his training coming into play with every polite smile he offered and every glass of champagne he delivered.

Though his duties were clear, the gallery felt different tonight. The air itself seemed charged, every conversation around him laced with the kind of undercurrent that only those with the highest stakes could bring into such a room. There was something intoxicating about the whole setup, something in the way the guests floated through the space as if they were part of something grander than themselves.

He stood just beyond the main gallery space, pretending to be absorbed in a painting—a sharp, angular piece that seemed to slice through the air with its dark, vivid strokes. His eyes roamed over it, but his mind wasn't focused on the art. Instead, he found himself observing the people—how they reacted to the paintings, how they moved, the subtle interactions that told him far more than any spoken word could.

Despite his best efforts to blend in, Alex's gaze wandered over to **Camellia** as she moved gracefully through the crowd. There was a controlled elegance to her every step, and though she seemed utterly absorbed in her guests, he knew better than to underestimate her awareness. Camellia was always watching, always measuring. His pulse quickened, but he quickly masked it with a slow exhale, redirecting his attention back to the room.

His job here was clear. But *why* he was here—why Camellia had insisted on this arrangement—was something he hadn't fully figured out. She had made it clear, of course, that he was to serve as both a willing participant and an observer in her world. And he had agreed, driven by reasons that had started to blur together as he spent more time under her watchful eye.

The evening wore on, and the guests continued to mingle, their conversations drifting in and out of focus as Alex slipped into autopilot. He delivered drinks with a practiced hand, smiled politely, and did everything he could to remain inconspicuous. Yet there was a restlessness inside him, an unease that refused to be ignored.

It wasn't just the work that left him unsettled. It was the weight of the situation. The questions that had been hanging in the air between him and **Camellia** had started to feel heavier, harder to ignore. Every interaction, every glance exchanged, seemed loaded with meaning—meaning that he wasn't sure he was ready to confront.

His eyes flickered back to Camellia, watching her as she spoke to a small group of patrons. There was something about the way she commanded the room that stirred something in him, something he couldn't quite name. Was it admiration? Fear? A twisted sense of both? He wasn't sure.

The tension between them had always been there, simmering beneath the surface, and tonight it felt more palpable than ever. But it wasn't just Camellia's presence that was making him uneasy. It was the thought that the gallery—this world he was trying to navigate—might not be as it seemed.

As Alex approached another group of guests, offering a glass of champagne with a smile, his mind flashed back to the conversation he'd had with Kenji a few days ago. The words that had lingered with him since then—the quiet suggestion that there was more happening in this space than anyone realized.

He quickly pushed the thought away, focusing on his duties. *Stay focused. Just do your job.* But deep down, he couldn't shake the feeling that something was coming—something he wasn't prepared for, something that would force him to confront everything he had chosen to ignore about this world. About *Camellia.*

As the evening wore on, the gallery's atmosphere thickened with unspoken conversations. The soft clinking of glasses and the rustling of elegant attire filled the space, but beneath it all, an undercurrent of tension swirled. Guests moved between the art, lost in its beauty, but always aware that they were in the presence of something far more than just a collection of paintings. They were in Camellia's world.

Alex stood at the edge of it, his eyes constantly scanning, ensuring that the night stayed flawless. He was part of this world—yet never fully immersed in it. He caught fleeting glances of Camellia, how she weaved through the crowd with the grace of someone who was always in control. Always. But there was something different tonight, something hanging between them.

Camellia's gaze met his across the room. For a moment, he thought he saw a flicker of something—an acknowledgment of the distance between them. But it was gone as quickly as it had appeared. She turned away, and the room returned to its quiet hum.

The night ended without incident, but the feeling of anticipation never quite left. As the last of the guests filtered out, the lights in the gallery dimmed further, and Camellia stood near the exit, observing the empty space. Her plans were in motion. The evening had gone according to her design, and though no one could know it, the game was shifting once more.

She allowed herself a moment to linger, soaking in the satisfaction of a flawless event. But in the back of her mind, there was still that gnawing thought—Maris, Alex, Devereux. There were pieces yet to be put into place.

With a quiet breath, Camellia turned and left the gallery for the night, retiring to her penthouse, confident that the next steps were already on their way.

Chapter Six: Salt on Silk

The penthouse was quiet as Camellia stepped inside, the doors clicking shut behind her. The soft hum of the city below seemed distant now, replaced by the stillness of the space she had carefully crafted to reflect her taste, her power. The modern lines of the furniture, the muted tones of the décor—it was all a reflection of her meticulous control over her surroundings.

For a moment, she allowed herself a brief pause, standing just inside the door as she exhaled, letting the weight of the evening slowly lift from her shoulders. The gallery event had been a success, but even amidst the perfection, a ripple of tension lingered. A subtle unease she couldn't quite name, a thread of discomfort woven into the night.

It was nothing she couldn't manage. It always was. She thrived in moments like these, moments of uncertainty—because she knew how to bend them to her will. And tonight, there were no distractions. Only the next steps.

Turning away from the door, she walked toward the large glass windows, her heels clicking softly on the polished floor. The view of the city stretched before her—an endless sprawl of lights, each one a reflection of a different life, a different story. But tonight, her focus wasn't on the city. It was on the next move, the game yet to unfold.

She moved toward the small, sleek bar in the corner of the room, her fingers brushing against the familiar bottles of liquor. Pouring herself a drink, the amber liquid swirling in the glass, she lifted it to her lips. The burn was sharp, but it settled her. It cleared her mind and allowed her to refocus.

Camellia was never one to sit still for long. She thrived on movement, action, control. The gallery had been a performance, carefully executed, a small part of the much larger picture. But tonight, she was returning to the world that truly shaped her—the world where power was traded in whispers and promises. The world of the elite, where influence flowed as freely as the champagne in their glasses.

After finishing her drink, Camellia set the glass down with a soft clink and moved toward her closet. She had no time to waste. Her next destination was already decided. An event in the heart of the city, where only the most influential gathered. A place where nothing was as it seemed, where secrets were passed under the sheen of luxury. A place where she would reassert her presence.

The dress she chose was black, sleek, and simple, but the fabric shimmered in the light, catching the eye in all the right ways. It was elegant, seductive— just like her. She slipped into it effortlessly, the silk falling against her skin like a second layer. She studied herself in the mirror for a moment, adjusting the neckline, watching the way the fabric clung to her curves. She was ready.

The city was alive with its usual vibrancy as Camellia stepped out into the night. The air was cooler now, the streets lit by the soft glow of streetlights, but the energy in the air was palpable. It was always this way when she ventured out. People noticed. People watched. And she welcomed it.

Her car glided through the streets, the hum of the city surrounding her, as Camellia let herself slip into the rhythm of the night. There was no hesitation, no uncertainty. She had made her plans. Everything was in motion.

The car came to a smooth stop in front of the venue—a sleek, modern building that radiated exclusivity. She stepped out, her heels striking the pavement with deliberate confidence, the sound sharp against the quiet hum of the night. She moved toward the entrance, the atmosphere inside exactly as she expected: dimly lit, filled with the faint murmur of conversation, the clinking of glasses. The elite mingled, exchanging secrets, promises, and favors, their lives intertwined with the art of power.

But as she stepped into the room, she knew all eyes would eventually find her. The power was hers to command, and the night, like all the others before it, would unfold exactly as she had planned. She was the one they would all be watching. She always was.

The venue was everything Camellia expected and more. Sleek, polished, with an air of exclusivity that wrapped itself around her like a silk thread. The lighting was soft but deliberate, casting shadows that hinted at the intrigue of the evening. Glasses of champagne shimmered in delicate hands, the faint hum of conversation filling the space like a carefully curated symphony.

At first, the crowd seemed exactly as she anticipated—rich, powerful, influential—but tonight, there was something in the air, something subtle that shifted the atmosphere. The unspoken tension hung just out of reach, clinging to the edges of the night like the taste of a secret she hadn't yet uncovered. Camellia moved with practiced ease, her presence commanding, but her eyes were constantly scanning the room, cataloging every gesture, every interaction. There was nothing left to chance in her world. The guests, the conversations, the subtle dynamics—they were all part of the same game, and Camellia was always in control.

As she sipped her drink, her eyes landed on a familiar face across the room. Though she didn't know his name, she recognized him immediately. It was the man who had caused an interruption at one of her events weeks ago—right as she reunited with Maris. The night had been pivotal for her; Maris's return had been everything, and the chaos this man had brought only heightened the moment's intensity. At the time, she had dismissed him, a brief disruption in the flow of the evening. Yet, the memory of his presence lingered, as he had left a strange mark on the night. His quiet authority, his cool detachment—it wasn't the kind of disruption Camellia tolerated, but she had to admit, it had been memorable.

He was standing at the bar now, a glass of wine in hand, speaking with a group of patrons who appeared deeply engaged in whatever he was saying. His presence was quiet, commanding, his every word holding weight. There was something about him that didn't quite belong in the crowd—a sharpness, an underlying danger that she couldn't ignore.

Camellia's gaze lingered on him for a moment longer, her curiosity piqued, but she quickly turned her focus back to the task at hand. There was no time to entertain distractions tonight. She had more pressing matters. Tonight was about reasserting her dominance in this world, about making sure that all eyes would be on her by the end of the evening. She wouldn't let anyone steal her spotlight—not now, not when she had already set everything in motion.

As the night wore on, the crowd thickened, and the buzz of conversation grew louder. Camellia moved from one guest to another, engaging in witty exchanges, her charm and poise evident to everyone who spoke with her. But her mind kept drifting back to the man at the bar—the one who had been responsible for the momentary disruption that had, in the end, heightened the drama of the night she had reunited with Maris. This man, Luciano, had done nothing to get in her way, but his mere presence felt like a test she wasn't prepared for. She watched him again, still there, still quiet, still unaware of her scrutiny. But the feeling in her chest remained—his calm detachment was more unsettling than she cared to admit.

The event was sponsored by Mr. Devereux, a name that had become synonymous with power and influence in the art world. Camellia knew him only on the surface—an art dealer with a smooth reputation, hosting exclusive events for the elite. He had circled her for years, always with the same goal: to claim Galerie Solé for his own. But Camellia had no intention of handing it over.

Their exchanges had always been playful, even witty—he made his subtle moves, and she parried with equal finesse. He was impressed by her strength, the way she always seemed to leave everyone she met in awe. But with Devereux, it was different. His admiration had always been skin-deep. She had long seen through the mask. Beneath it, he was tired of games, tired of pretending that their little dance didn't leave him hungry for more than just a flirtation with power.

Camellia could sense the shift in his demeanor tonight. His charming smile could no longer disguise the hunger in his eyes. Mr. Devereux wasn't here to play games. He was here to take what he believed should be his. And Camellia wasn't going to make it easy for him.

As the evening came to a close, the venue began to empty out. The elite filtered out, slipping into their luxurious cars, their conversations now intimate, their secrets shared behind closed doors. Camellia stood near the entrance, observing the last of the guests depart. A sense of satisfaction washed over her. The event had been a success, at least on the surface. She had played her part. She had maintained her control.

But just as she prepared to leave, she saw him again.

Luciano.

He was still by the bar, no longer speaking with anyone, but instead quietly observing the remaining guests. Their eyes met across the room, and there was no mistaking the recognition in his gaze. Still, he didn't approach her. Instead, he gave her a slight nod—a silent acknowledgment of sorts—but continued minding his business.

For a moment, Camellia considered walking toward him, but the thought passed. It wasn't the time. She didn't need distractions. He was no threat. Still, something in the way he carried himself intrigued her, and for a heartbeat longer than usual, her gaze lingered on him.

But without another word, he turned, disappearing back into the crowd. Camellia remained still, her curiosity unfulfilled, but her control unwavering. Tonight had been about maintaining her position, and she had done so flawlessly.

The night was almost over. But as the last of the guests filtered into the streets, Camellia felt the weight of something else building. There were pieces moving in the background, and the real game hadn't even begun.

The cool night air wrapped itself around Camellia as she stepped into her penthouse, the sound of her heels clicking sharply against the polished marble floor. The city's hum was a distant murmur, almost drowned out by the quiet stillness of the apartment. Tonight had unfolded exactly as planned—the power moves, the subtle shifts—all of it had placed her one step closer to her goals. Yet, as she crossed the threshold, the satisfaction of the evening began to fade, replaced by a subtle, unsettling calm.

She hadn't expected anyone to be here. But as she entered the kitchen, her eyes immediately locked onto the figure sitting at the table.

Maris.

The sight of her sitting there, relaxed with a drink in hand, was unexpected but not unwelcome. Her posture was casual, her confidence almost tangible in the air around her. The smile she gave Camellia was soft, knowing, and there was something about it—a flicker of pride, a touch of defiance—that tugged at Camellia's chest.

For a moment, the tension of the night seemed to dissipate. But there was something different about Maris now—something in the way she sat, a subtle shift in the power dynamic between them. The feeling was immediate and undeniable: Maris had returned with a newfound air of confidence. She had been away for some time, completing a job that had taken her out of Camellia's orbit, and now, she stood before her, no longer the woman Camellia had once carefully molded.

Maris had returned, not just physically, but mentally—she had changed. There was a quiet certainty about her now, an unspoken authority that Camellia couldn't ignore.

Camellia didn't move at first, studying her from the doorway. Maris didn't budge either, simply holding her gaze, her fingers absently swirling the drink in her hand, as if she had all the time in the world.

The sound of the door softly closing behind her felt heavier than it should have. Camellia's breath caught for just a moment, a faint flutter of uncertainty hidden beneath the otherwise impenetrable composure.

"I didn't expect you to be here," Camellia finally said, her voice controlled, but the weight of their shared history thickened the air between them.

Maris's smile deepened, her eyes glinting with a quiet intensity that Camellia knew well. "I figured you'd be busy," she replied, voice soft yet carrying an edge Camellia hadn't heard in quite some time. "But you're never too busy for me, are you?"

There it was. The first crack in the carefully crafted shell between them. Maris had always been her muse, her creation—but now she had become something different. The shift was subtle, but it was there, an undercurrent of power that hadn't been there before. Camellia's grip on her drink tightened slightly. She could feel it: the change in the balance between them.

"I had some things to take care of," Camellia responded coolly, though her gaze remained fixed on Maris. The words weren't a dismissal—they never were. But her mind was already on the next step, the next move. There was no room for distractions tonight. Not now, not after everything that had transpired.

Maris leaned back in her chair, unfazed, her eyes locked on Camellia's with an almost lazy amusement. "You've been keeping busy, I see," she mused, her voice low, yet laced with an edge of something darker. "It's been a long time, hasn't it?"

The words lingered in the air. A full year. Since Maris had left the first time. The silence that followed had been sharp. Camellia hadn't expected her return so soon after her departure the other night—her absence had been a wound before, a scar she'd never fully allowed to heal. But in the silence of their separation, Camellia had built herself up again since then. She had refined her power, her control, but now that Maris was back, there was a crack forming in that foundation, a reminder of the woman she had once been, without control. She refused to be that woman again.

The night they had been torn apart had been devastating, but it had been necessary. Maris had left to complete a job—a job that had been more important than their relationship, than everything between them. That was how Camellia justified the hurt, but the truth was darker. There was no replacing the hole left when Maris walked away, not until tonight.

"Too long," Camellia replied, her voice steady but carrying an undercurrent of something she wasn't willing to acknowledge. Her movements were slow, deliberate, as she took a step closer to the table, her eyes never leaving Maris. The tension between them crackled in the space. The weight of their shared history—the push, the pull, the control—hung between them like a silent challenge.

Maris's smile softened, but the defiance in her eyes remained. She was no longer the fragile muse Camellia had shaped to her will in recent weeks. She had become something more—a woman with her own power, her own purpose. And that change... that was what Camellia had been both afraid and excited to face.

"Well," Maris said, breaking the silence, her voice soft but with an unspoken intensity, "I'm not going anywhere. Not tonight, anyway."

The words hung in the air, pregnant with meaning. A promise. A challenge. It stirred something deep within Camellia—a recognition of the shift, a realization that she no longer held all the cards. Not in the same way she had previously.

"Good," Camellia replied, her voice low, smooth, and controlled. But her gaze was unwavering. "I didn't think you would."

For a brief moment, they simply stood there, caught in a dance of subtle power, each one measuring the other. Neither of them willing to admit the full weight of what had shifted. But both of them fully aware that something had changed.

And tonight, the tension between them was no longer just about control—it was about ownership. The dance had shifted, and they were no longer the same players they had been when they first started.

The silence between them deepened, charged with an electricity that was impossible to ignore. Camellia felt the familiar rush of adrenaline she always experienced when faced with Maris, the woman who could shatter her composure with just a look. It was the same feeling that had unsettled her a year ago, the one she hadn't been able to shake since the night Maris had walked away without a word.

But now, the game had changed.

Camellia stepped closer to the table, the rhythm of her breath slowing, her eyes never leaving Maris. The sharp, controlled movements she had mastered in every other part of her life seemed to dissolve in this space, leaving something raw, something unspoken between them. It wasn't just the physical distance between them that had closed. It was the emotional divide.

Maris stood, her lips curling into a smile that was both inviting and teasing, her gaze locked onto Camellia with a knowing intensity. She took a step toward her, moving with the fluid grace of someone who knew exactly what they wanted—and how to take it.

"You seem different," Camellia murmured, the words slipping out before she could stop them. "Confident. Unyielding like when we met. It suits you."

Maris tilted her head, the flicker of a challenge in her eyes. She stepped closer, closing the gap between them, her breath warm against Camellia's skin. "You made me that way," she said, her voice low, thick with meaning.

The words hung in the air, their weight heavier than any spoken before.

Camellia's heart beat faster, the pulse of her desire rising as Maris moved even closer, her lips now just inches from hers. Every breath, every subtle movement between them seemed to burn with the anticipation of what was about to unfold.

"I've wanted this," Camellia confessed, her voice a whisper that was lost in the space between them. "I've always wanted this."

Before Camellia could fully process the heat of the words, Maris's hands were on her, pulling her closer. The touch was soft but insistent, sending a jolt of electricity through Camellia's body. The weight of Maris's touch, the warmth of her skin against Camellia's, ignited a fire that had been smoldering beneath the surface for far too long.

A soft sigh escaped Camellia's lips as she leaned into the kiss that Maris initiated. It was slow, deliberate, but it quickly deepened, their lips moving together with a hunger that neither of them could suppress. Camellia's hands roamed to Maris's back, pulling her closer, feeling the familiar warmth of her body, the soft silk of her dress slipping beneath Camellia's fingers.

Maris responded in kind, her hands tracing the curve of Camellia's neck, tilting her head to deepen the kiss. The heat between them grew, and in that moment, there was nothing else—no gallery, no distractions. Just the two of them, bound by something that couldn't be put into words.

Camellia's breath caught as Maris pulled away just enough to look into her eyes, the intensity of her gaze sending a rush of heat through Camellia's body. "You've always controlled this, haven't you?" Maris whispered, her voice thick with both challenge and desire.

Camellia's smile was slow, confident. "Only because you let me," she replied, her lips brushing against Maris's with every word.

The challenge between them was undeniable. And yet, in this moment, it was the very thing that fueled the passion igniting between them. Maris was no longer just a muse. She had become something more—a force Camellia couldn't fully control, and yet, a force she craved to dominate once again.

Without warning, Maris took control, her hands sliding down Camellia's sides as she kissed her again, this time with more urgency, a deep, frantic need. Camellia gasped against her lips, her body responding, heat pooling in the pit of her stomach. She didn't fight it—she couldn't. Every touch, every movement between them sent waves of sensation through her body, breaking down every last bit of restraint.

As the kiss deepened, the world around them began to fade. Camellia's mind was clouded with desire, her body fully attuned to Maris's touch. The pull between them was magnetic, undeniable, and as their bodies pressed closer together, Camellia knew that this was what had always been meant to happen. This was the culmination of everything they had been through—the games, the tension, the separation.

Nothing else mattered now.

Maris's hands were on Camellia's dress, the fabric sliding down her shoulders, leaving her skin exposed to the cool air. But the sensation of Maris's hands on her, the touch that felt like fire, was all Camellia could focus on. Her own hands, guided by desire and instinct, found their way to Maris's dress, tugging it off her with a mix of tenderness and urgency.

And when they finally came together again, skin to skin, the world outside the penthouse seemed to disappear entirely.

They were locked in each other's embrace, lost in a moment that was as much about surrender as it was about dominance. Camellia, once the one in control, felt herself losing that control, and yet, it felt like freedom. And for Maris, the woman who had once walked away, she now stood before Camellia, an equal, no longer bound by the delicate threads of power that had once ruled them both.

Their bodies moved together in perfect rhythm, a dance they had always known how to perform, but one that had taken on a new intensity tonight. The tension, the pull, the longing—it was all coming to a head, and there was no turning back.

The world outside the penthouse faded into the quiet hum of the city, leaving only the two of them. Camellia's heart beat in time with the restless energy of the night as Maris leaned in, her presence a slow-burning flame that enveloped her, pulling her deeper into the warmth of a desire Camellia had tried to suppress. Every inch of their skin seemed to burn as they finally came together, the weight of the past, the sting of distance, melting into the present.

Their kiss began slow, deliberate, an almost teasing brush of lips that carried the taste of old memories—sweet, bitter, and full of everything that had gone unsaid between them. Camellia could feel the hunger in Maris's kiss, the ache of a reunion long overdue. There was no room for hesitation anymore. There was only the pull between them, the unspoken need, desperate and undeniable.

Maris's hands slid up Camellia's back, fingers tracing the sensitive line of her spine, sending shivers of pleasure that seemed to echo through Camellia's entire body. The touch was light at first, teasing—testing the waters—but it quickly deepened, becoming more insistent, more urgent. Maris wasn't just touching her. She was claiming her, and in that moment, Camellia understood: Maris had returned as a force of her own. She was no longer a muse to be shaped. She was a woman to be reckoned with.

The kiss deepened, and Camellia's hands found Maris's face, cupping it gently before pulling her even closer. The heat between them was unmistakable, a spark that ignited something primal, something raw. Maris's breath came faster as their bodies pressed together, the soft rise and fall of their chests moving in sync. Every brush of skin, every touch, was like an electric current connecting them in a way nothing else could.

When Maris pulled back slightly, her lips brushed against Camellia's ear as she whispered, "I'm not the same as before. I'm not the same woman that left you behind."

The words echoed in Camellia's mind, vibrating deep within her. She wanted to speak, to answer, but all she could do was close the distance between them once more, pulling Maris back into the kiss. Her hands roamed, tracing the soft, familiar lines of Maris's body, but this time, it was different. Maris had become something more—something powerful, something capable of giving as much as she took.

The sudden motion of Maris undressing her was a shock to Camellia, but it wasn't unwelcome. Maris's fingers slid down the zipper of Camellia's dress with practiced ease, revealing more skin, inch by inch, until the fabric slipped away completely. The sensation was electric. Each movement was a delicate undoing, like a slow dance of surrender and reclamation. Camellia stood exposed before her, heart pounding in her chest, breath shallow, and the heat between them building to a fever pitch.

Maris didn't waste time. She was in no hurry, but the intensity of her movements was undeniable. Her hands moved with a confident tenderness, one that made Camellia's pulse quicken with every touch. Maris wasn't just claiming her body. She was discovering it again, as if learning the familiar terrain of her skin for the first time, teasing, exploring, unwrapping every layer Camellia had so carefully hidden.

Camellia's hands slid down to Maris's waist, feeling the soft curve of her hips, pulling her closer as their bodies collided with a sense of urgency that had been too long in the making. Their lips found each other again, this time with an insatiable hunger. Every kiss was deep, fevered, as if they were trying to drink from each other, as if they could never get enough. The need, the craving, was overwhelming.

In the dim light of the penthouse, nothing existed but Maris and Camellia, their bodies tangled together, their movements synchronized in an intimate dance that spoke louder than words ever could. Camellia's hands moved along Maris's back, tracing the lines of her shoulders, feeling the tautness of her muscles, the heat of her skin beneath her fingertips. She felt it—Maris had always been this close, but now she was something else entirely: no longer just a muse, but a force of nature, unapologetic, wild, and beautiful.

The tension between them grew unbearable, and without another word, Maris guided Camellia to the couch, their bodies tumbling together, crashing into the soft cushions. There was no room for anything else now. No more games, no more boundaries. They moved together, effortlessly, as if they had always known this rhythm, this connection. The sounds of the night outside faded, leaving only the soft rustling of fabric and the breathless whispers between them.

Maris's hands found their way to Camellia's body again, exploring every inch with a hunger that was both possessive and tender. Maris kissed her with abandon, her lips trailing a fiery path down Camellia's neck, her body pressed firmly against Camellia's as if she couldn't get close enough. The way

Maris moved, the way she touched Camellia—it was a conversation of its own, one that needed no words. It was an unraveling, a mutual surrender.

And as their bodies came together again, this time with an intensity that shook them both, Camellia finally understood. It wasn't just about power anymore. It was about being with someone who could match her, someone who could leave her breathless, lost, and whole all at once.

The night was theirs, and nothing else mattered. Nothing else could reach them in this moment.

The couch welcomed them like an altar of ruin and reverence—where all that had been withheld, wounded, or whispered between them now demanded release. Their mouths collided again, less like a kiss and more like a reclamation—of time, of memory, of power lost and returned.

Camellia felt the shift the moment Maris took control of her lower lip, tugging it gently before deepening the kiss with a hunger sharpened by absence. Camellia had always been the conductor, the orchestrator of every beat—but now she was the one being unmade. And it thrilled her. Her breath caught when Maris's hand gripped her thigh with unexpected authority, spreading her beneath her weight, anchoring her.

She's not the same girl, Camellia thought wildly, her nails grazing Maris's shoulders as silk and control slipped away in equal measure.

She came back changed.

She came back to claim me.

From Maris's perspective, every inch of Camellia beneath her was a storm rediscovered. The smooth, expensive skin she once worshipped now trembled with need, and it wasn't fear—it was surrender. Camellia's neck arched as Maris kissed her way down, teeth grazing the hollow of her throat, her hands exploring the ridges of a body she'd memorized, rewritten, and missed like air.

"I remember," Maris murmured against her collarbone, her voice velvet and wild. "I remember how to break you apart."

Camellia shivered beneath her, caught between a gasp and a laugh. "Do it, then."

Their clothing gave way in layers, each removal deliberate, a revelation.

Maris's dress was completely gone, revealing the body that had haunted Camellia's dreams for a year—a body that danced between power and abandon. Camellia, in return, unzipped her own façade, baring the curve of her breasts, the lines of her hips, the heat already blooming low in her belly.

They met again, flesh to flesh.

Hands roamed. Tongues teased. Breath hitched and tangled.

Maris straddled her, their thighs sliding together in a rhythm older than language. Camellia's hands gripped her waist, guiding, then letting go. Their eyes met as their bodies rocked against one another—heat building, friction exquisite. It was a battlefield of pleasure and pride, and neither would yield entirely.

Maris gasped when Camellia's nails dug into her back, sharp and claiming. "Still possessive?"

"Always," Camellia whispered, tilting her hips to meet Maris's rhythm with a roll that stole both their breaths.

But then, Maris leaned down, her lips brushing Camellia's ear, her fingers sliding between their bodies, finding her with unerring precision.

"Then you better show me," she whispered, breath hot and cruelly tender, "before I make you beg."

Camellia's retort was lost in a moan—sharp, real, ragged.

From there, it was a slow unraveling.

Camellia flipped them with a growl, her body pinning Maris beneath her, reclaiming her throne with a sensual ferocity. She trailed kisses down Maris's torso, her tongue flicking the edges of her nipple, then sucking until Maris writhed beneath her, fingers tangled in dark curls, breathing broken.

And then lower—Camellia's mouth found her center, and Maris's hips lifted in raw need, her thighs parting without question. Camellia devoured her like vengeance and prayer, steady and devastating, until Maris cried out a name she hadn't dared say in months. Her thighs trembled. Her back arched. But still Camellia didn't let up.

Maris came undone with a cry, her entire body arching like a bow, but when the wave passed, she didn't retreat.

She pulled Camellia up, kissed her, tasted herself on her lover's tongue, and whispered, "Now lie back."

And Camellia did.

For once, she surrendered completely—body taut with anticipation, thighs glistening, breath shallow. Maris knelt between her legs, her hands parting her slowly, reverently. Camellia gasped when Maris's tongue found her—slow at first, then devastatingly exact. Her fingers gripped the cushions. Her hips bucked. Her voice trembled.

They fell again and again—into one another's mouths, their arms, their dominance and vulnerability.

It wasn't just sex.

It was confession.

It was penance.

It was carnal.

By the time their bodies finally stilled, Camellia lay atop Maris, their breaths tangled, their sweat cooling against the high-thread-count decadence of her couch. Neither of them spoke. They didn't need to. Everything that needed to be said had been translated through tongue, touch, and the way they both refused to let go.

Chapter Seven: The Archivist's Secret

The morning sun broke over Île Seguin like a whispered confession, light spilling across the penthouse windows in long, deliberate streaks. Camellia awoke alone. The sheets still held the warmth of Maris's body, a trace of scent that lingered like a memory pressed into silk. But Maris was gone. Again.

And yet—there was no ache, no panic.

Instead, a slow smile curved her lips.

She stretched languidly across the bed, her body humming with residual electricity. The night before had been one of those rare moments where the world peeled back and revealed something raw, something beautiful. There had been laughter muffled against skin, whispered provocations, promises sealed in the dark. There had been no masks, no power games—only breathless confessions whispered against her collarbone and fingers tangled in hair.

The absence this time did not feel like a wound. It felt like trust.

She reached over to the untouched side of the bed, dragging her hand along the still-warm sheets. Her eyes fluttered shut, and for one suspended breath, she allowed herself to bask in it. The scent of Maris—jasmine, sandalwood, and something sweetly defiant—still lingered in the pillows. Camellia breathed it in deeply, memorizing the comfort of it, the weightless pleasure of knowing that Maris had returned not in apology—but in power.

She didn't need a note. Didn't need a reason. The quiet said it all.

Camellia slid from the bed, her bare feet touching the cool marble floor as she wrapped herself in a black silk robe. It shimmered as she moved, hugging the curves of a body still tender with memory. Every step was languid, unrushed. She poured herself a cup of coffee, letting the rich aroma bloom around her. The first sip was grounding, bitter and bold—the perfect counterbalance to the sweetness she still felt coursing through her veins.

A soft laugh escaped her lips as she turned to face the morning light, her reflection caught faintly in the floor-to-ceiling windows. She looked like someone in possession of something sacred. And she was.

There was work to do. Yes. But for the first time in a long while, it didn't feel like an escape.

It felt like momentum.

She padded barefoot into her study, the sanctum she rarely let others see. Shelves lined with curated archives, documents, photographs, and things far more delicate than truth. This room was her power, her secret world of control. But something was wrong.

One of the archive drawers sat slightly ajar. She dragged her fingers across the edge of the drawer, past familiar folders and meticulously labeled entries—until one stopped her cold. A single header. No details. Just a name, printed in thin serif caps across a red-stamped label:

DELPHINIUM

She hadn't seen it in years. Hadn't dared open it. Not even after the fire. Especially not after the fire.

Camellia paused mid-sip. The tightening in her chest had nothing to do with caffeine. She set the cup down gently and crossed the room. Her fingers hovered above the drawer—third row, second from the left. The one she never touched unless absolutely necessary.

Inside, a small black velvet box lay open atop a sheet of crisp parchment. The contents were unnervingly precise—a flash drive, faded black-and-white photographs, and a time-worn, hand-written letter tucked into an envelope marked with her family seal.

But the seal was broken.

A surge of ice flooded her spine. She hadn't placed it there. And she hadn't let anyone else in. Which meant someone had been here. Someone had violated her sanctuary—not with violence, but with intention. Precision. They hadn't ransacked the place. They hadn't left signs of forced entry. No, this was worse. Far worse.

Whoever had done this had known exactly what they were looking for—and where to put it so it would be found.

The flash drive sat in the center like an invitation. The photographs—grainy and yellowed—showed people she recognized. Her father. A younger version of her mother. An unnamed figure in the background, always present, always watching. The letter, creased and delicate, seemed to hum with unspoken warnings.

Camellia picked it up with care, heart pounding louder than the city outside her window. The envelope had once been sealed with the Solé crest—a sigil rarely used, and only for blood-bound matters. Its breach meant something ancient had been disturbed.

The air around her grew heavier as she unfolded the letter. The ink had bled in places, watermarked by time and perhaps tears. But it was the handwriting—delicate, resolute—that made her fingers tremble. Whoever had written it knew the family. Intimately. Lines curled around secrets she hadn't yet named, questions she had buried in favor of control.

A sharp knock at the front door shattered the thick silence like glass. It rang through the space with an eerie clarity, like a judge's gavel before a verdict. It didn't echo—it throbbed, like a heartbeat on the other side of something unspeakable.

Camellia turned, the letter still in her hand. The city below whispered on, unaware. But she was no longer part of its rhythm. Not now.

She moved to answer it, every step an echo of calculated calm, though her pulse thundered beneath her skin. Something felt wrong. Not just in the drawer, not just in the intrusion—but in the knock itself. Too sharp. Too perfectly timed.

On the other side stood Vivianne.

"We have a problem," she said without preamble.

Camellia raised a brow. "Only one?"

Vivianne handed her a manila folder. Inside were photographs. Surveillance stills. One of Maris. One of a man Camellia didn't recognize.

"They were sent anonymously," Vivianne continued. "Dropped through a secure channel. Whoever sent them wanted us to know someone's been watching. But more than that—they wanted you to see who's moving in your shadow."

Camellia's breath caught. Not because of what was in the folder—but because of what wasn't.

Each photo came with a dossier, printed in the same plain formatting used in internal intelligence reports. Camellia's eyes skimmed through—dates, locations, timestamps. But most of the information was blacked out. Entire sections of background, origin, even names in some cases. Redacted. Sanitized. As if whoever compiled them wanted her to know just enough—and no more.

Mr. Devereux wouldn't be so bold. Not yet. He was a predator who disguised himself as a gentleman, a collector of power who cloaked his threats in velvet and charm. He'd coveted Galerie Solé for years, circling it like a fox at the edge of the woods. But Camellia would never entertain an alliance with him—and he would never support her unless it served her ruin.

Which meant this wasn't his move.

She glanced back toward the still-open drawer, the broken seal, the unspoken message embedded in the artifacts. Someone had breached her sanctum. Someone who knew where to strike.

Deliberate.

Intimate.

Invasive.

Every detail had been surgical. The placement. The contents. The timing. The flash drive. The letter. The broken seal.

A chess move.

The air felt colder now. The shadows in the corners of the penthouse seemed to inch closer, pressing inward like a secret tightening its grip. The light that poured in moments before now felt watchful, exposing. She clenched the folder tighter in her hand as a tremor of rage threatened to rise. Not just fear—violation. Whoever had done this wasn't just digging into her past. They were rewriting it. Reframing it. Turning her family's legacy into a weapon against her.

And they were close. Closer than she had ever allowed anyone to be.

She took a slow breath, forcing the stillness back into her limbs. The game had changed.

And somewhere out there, the archivist who once preserved her past... might now be curating her downfall.

She turned back to the drawer, the letter still trembling in her hand.

"Leave me," she said softly.

Vivianne didn't protest. She simply nodded once, her footsteps retreating down the marble hall like a curtain falling over the final scene.

Only once she was alone did Camellia allow herself to sit. She smoothed the envelope across her desk, fingers tracing the raised remnants of the Solé seal. Whatever waited inside had survived time, betrayal, and silence.

Her eyes scanned the letter:

The past is not buried. It waits. Just like I did.

What is sought is older than the gallery. Older than the name it serves. Follow the scent of ash and rose. It will lead you to the beginning.

You are not the first to inquire. But you may be the last to decide.

Some archives were never meant to be opened.

The name at the top—faded, smeared—was no longer legible. Worn down by time, by hands that once folded it closed, perhaps in grief, perhaps in warning.

No signature. No date. Just that cryptic whisper, etched in time.

Her breath caught. The handwriting—slanted, looping—was achingly familiar. It couldn't be. Not her. Not after all these years. But something in her chest clawed upward, whispering a name she had buried with fire and silence: Dhalia.

She turned the envelope over again, inspecting its edges, trying to place how someone had gotten this deep. Her building had no gaps. Her locks, her security, her routines—nothing left to chance. And still... they had come.

And they had left only this: a message without a sender, a warning without a voice, a letter addressed to a ghost—and now read by the heir to everything they once protected... or betrayed.

Camellia remained seated at her desk, the letter still unfurled before her, when the silence of the room returned to full weight. Every sound was amplified—the ticking of a nearby clock, the faint groan of the building settling, the distant honk of a river ferry below. Yet inside her chest, everything had gone still.

She reached for the photographs again, dragging the manila folder across the desk. Maris. The unknown man. Tracked with deliberate intent. Whoever was watching wasn't new to this game. They were tracing connections Camellia had only just begun to acknowledge herself. The people closest to her were no longer just confidants—they were liabilities. Or lures.

She closed her eyes.

She saw the inked script burned behind her lids, the scent of ash and rose curling in her senses like smoke from an invisible fire. Somewhere, someone was counting on her to follow it. To step directly into the embers.

She stood abruptly, her chair gliding back with a sharp sigh against the floor. The letter she folded carefully, precisely, and tucked back into its envelope. But she did not return it to the drawer.

No. This would stay with her now.

There was no more hiding from the past.

There was only the descent into it.

And she would go willingly, if not warily—into the dark, into the forgotten, into the fire that had once forged her bloodline and now threatened to consume it whole.

The shadows waited.

And she would meet them.

She moved from the study in silence, her feet gliding over cool marble as she entered her bedroom once more. Her robe slipped from her shoulders with a whisper, pooling to the floor like spilled ink. She stepped beneath the rainfall showerhead in her private bath, water cascading over her in steaming sheets. Her fingers moved with slow intent, gliding over her chest, lathering the jasmine soap in soft circles over each breast, the water tracing the path of her knuckles as they slid lower across her stomach. She lingered a moment at her pelvis, the heat and pressure making her draw a deeper breath, then worked the suds between her thighs with a grace that was more ritual than routine.

She reached for the exfoliant scrub next, massaging it into her arms and collarbone, working methodically down to her thighs and calves. Steam cloaked her like silk, veiling her in softness that contrasted the storm she knew was coming. She shampooed and rinsed her hair in slow, practiced motions, eyes closed, mind sharpening with every pass of her fingers. When she finally let herself lean into the stream, she imagined it washing away more than memory—she imagined it baptizing her into whatever came next.

The hot water beat against her nape and back, pulsing down like absolution. She closed her eyes beneath the deluge, palms pressed flat to the tile, jaw tight with resolve. The scent of jasmine soap swirled with something colder—memory, maybe. Or foreshadow.

When she emerged, she was heat-flushed and gleaming, wrapped in a towel that clung to her form as steam ghosted from her limbs. Her eyes, no longer soft from sleep, had sharpened.

She stepped into the adjoining dressing chamber. Her movements were fluid, deliberate. She selected black silk panties, seamless and high-waisted—minimal coverage, maximum control. Over them, she clipped a lace garter belt with hidden fasteners, matching it with sheer thigh-highs that whispered against her skin as she smoothed them into place.

Her bra was ivory—structured, tailored, lifting. A contrast to the severity of her trousers and the crisp perfection of the ivory silk blouse she buttoned with care. Her heels were matte black stilettos, sleek and silent.

As she adjusted her cuffs, she paged for her assistant:

"Vivianne."

A beat later, Vivianne appeared in the doorway, composed but alert.

Camellia didn't turn. "We'll need access to the outer registry—off-grid entries from the past month. Cross-reference them with the timestamps from the photographs."

Vivianne nodded. "I'll have it ready within the hour. And I'll loop in our encrypted archive team in case anything from the old grid pings."

Camellia reached for her earrings—obsidian studs, the kind that never drew attention but recorded everything. "And flag the unknown male in the dossier. I want to know what we're not being told. Every angle. Every inconsistency."

"Understood," Vivianne replied. "And what about Maris?"

Camellia paused mid-motion, then continued securing her cuffs. Her voice was velvet over steel. "We don't act. Not yet. Just… watch. If this is meant to draw me in, I'll walk willingly. But not blindly."

Vivianne took a measured step forward, her gaze intense. "Who do you think is behind this?"

Camellia turned her head slightly. "I don't know, but we're no longer in control of the narrative—we're playing a part in someone else's curation."

Vivianne's breath caught. "Then I'll prepare the descent. Quietly."

Camellia nodded once. "And if anything surfaces—anything—we pivot. No attachments. No assumptions."

Vivianne's lips curved into the faintest smile. "You taught me that."

Camellia gave her a final glance, a quiet vow hanging in the space between them: "No more shadows without light."

And she stepped into the day not as prey—but as the storm gathering on the edge of its horizon.

Chapter Eight: Smoke in the Halls

The day unfolded with an eerie stillness, as if the city itself knew it was being watched. From the panoramic windows of Galerie Solé, the Seine shimmered beneath an overcast sky, its surface disrupted only by the slow churn of tourist boats and the occasional call of gulls. The gallery was not yet open to the public, but the staff moved like clockwork through its cavernous halls—each step, each whisper, restrained and calculated.

Camellia stood at the mezzanine rail, her gaze sweeping over the atrium below. Today, the space felt different. The light fractured strangely through the overhead glass, casting long, uncertain shadows on the pristine marble floor. Even the art on the walls seemed more watchful, more severe.

She had not told anyone about the letter. Or the photographs. Or the dossier that still burned like ice in her private bag.

Vivianne trailed behind her, notepad in hand, speaking quietly. "Security rotation has been tightened. I've added two plainclothes agents near the west wing and repositioned the motion sensors to cover blind angles. No red flags yet, but there's a pattern forming."

Camellia didn't look at her. Her fingers curled around the edge of the rail, nails pressing faint crescents into her palm. "Define the pattern."

Vivianne flipped a page. "Whoever's been watching isn't just tracking Maris or the unknown male. They're tracking proximity. Appearances. Emotional frequency. How often someone enters your sphere, how long they linger. How your mood shifts after. It's not surveillance—it's orchestration."

Camellia's jaw tightened. "A curator's eye."

"Or a puppeteer's."

She turned from the mezzanine, descending the stairs in measured, unhurried steps. Her heels struck marble with crisp finality. She moved like smoke through the gallery—graceful, composed, untouchable—but with every step, her thoughts twisted tighter.

She passed a wall-sized triptych in crimson and obsidian, an abstract of grief and resurrection by a Japanese artist whose past had been erased by war. It had always spoken to her. Today, it whispered something new.

Beneath her calm exterior, something ancient stirred.

Vivianne caught up again. "Do we activate the archival sweep? Cross-reference the handwriting from the letter?"

"No. Not yet. Whoever sent it is expecting curiosity."

"Then what do we do?"

Camellia stopped at the foot of the main stairwell, gaze lifting toward the vaulted ceiling. "We let the hall breathe. We let them think we're still asleep."

Vivianne hesitated, then nodded. "Understood."

Camellia's voice dropped to a whisper. "But don't blink. Not for a second. Smoke doesn't just rise, Vivianne. It chokes before it warns."

Not far from the gallery, parked on a narrow rue with tinted windows dimming the world beyond, Maris sat in silence.

The interior of the car was dark, soundproofed, and sterile. She wore a matte black earpiece, barely visible beneath her waves of hair. On her lap, a sleek tablet flickered with encrypted light. Her fingers moved in calculated rhythms, tracing patterns of surveillance, pings of communication—and then a connection spiked. A call intercepted.

She tapped in. Masked frequencies, ghosted routing. The speaker's voice came through distorted—mechanical, synthetic. A modulated blend of tones designed to protect identity.

But Maris knew exactly who it was.

Kenji.

"Report," came the voice, low and flat, but edged with command.

There was hesitation on the other end. Then Alex's voice—slightly hoarse, uncertain. "I... I haven't had a full sitrep. Timing's been—complicated."

Kenji's pause was thunderous. "You've missed three check-ins, Alex. You're deviating."

"I've been managing proximity," Alex replied, tone defensive but fraying. "Camellia—she's unpredictable. I needed to stay embedded."

Another long silence. Then: "Unpredictable doesn't negate protocol. You were not sent to improvise. You were sent to observe, to report. What part of that did your fascination override?"

Alex's reply was a breath, not a word. Shame, exposed and raw.

"Has she seen the contents?"

"Yes. She's... rattled. Trying to mask it, but it's there."

Kenji's voice lowered. "And what of your own mask, Alex? Or has she already peeled that off, too?"

Alex said nothing.

"You're compromised. Your silence says as much."

Alex finally replied, voice quiet. "What do you want me to do?"

"Nothing. For now. You've done enough damage."

Another silence.

"And Maris?"

Kenji's tone shifted. "Still watching. Still listening. She's your next shadow, whether you see her or not. Tread lightly, Alex. She doesn't clean up other people's messes—she buries them."

The call ended with a click sharp as a blade drawn in the dark.

Maris exhaled slowly and leaned back against the leather seat, her gaze fixed on her own reflection in the tinted window.

Her voice barely moved past her lips. "You poor, beautiful fool."

She closed the tablet, the screen going black as the space around her. The encryption terminated, but the consequences would echo.

She didn't need to find Alex.

He would come to her.

And when he did, he would learn—

She was never just the dancer.

She was the reckoning.

Far from the eyes of Camellia, deeper in the digital ether, Kenji moved like shadow and current.

Alone in a private blacksite server chamber miles outside Paris, he stood before a trio of silent monitors, each aglow with overlapping network trees and cascading lines of decrypted data. His fingers danced across a silent mechanical keyboard, inputting strings of code designed to bypass Galerie Solé's custom-built security layers.

Camellia's system was a fortress—beautifully constructed, armored with false paths and phantom keys. But nothing built by human hands was impenetrable.

Kenji had slipped through firewalls like breath through silk. What he needed wasn't brute access.

It was silence.

Every ping was disguised. Every trace was folded into gallery maintenance logs and internal latency. What would appear as nothing more than a system recalibration was, in truth, a quiet excavation.

Camellia's internal files were curated like the gallery itself—artful, pristine, and misleading. But beneath the veneer, he began to find fragments. Redacted estate records. Incomplete adoption inquiries. Financial donations under burner identities—funds traced back to the Solé family's ancestral holdings in Algiers, Rome, and Kyoto.

The gallery's founder archives had been accessed recently—by Camellia herself. She had lingered on a file with a name he didn't recognize. He flagged it immediately.

But it was the encrypted personal directory—shielded behind multi-factor sequences and biometric firewalls—that gave him pause.

She knew more than she let on.

Or worse—she knew less than she needed to.

Kenji leaned closer to the screen as a single file blinked to life beneath layers of obfuscation.

Marked only: *VEL SOLARIA.*

He didn't open it.

Not yet.

He wasn't afraid of what it would reveal.

He was afraid of who else might already be reading it.

Then something changed. A ripple in the signal. An anomaly.

Kenji's eyes narrowed as he opened a mirrored diagnostics window. Another presence had entered the network.

Not gallery staff. Not his own echo.

Someone else.

They moved with caution but without refinement—skilled, but impatient. They weren't using obfuscation protocols. No packet fragmentation. No shadow port redirection. They were moving like a thief with a flashlight, clever enough to unlock doors, but not smart enough to disarm the silent alarms waiting just beneath the floorboards.

They hadn't tripped anything—yet. But if they dug deeper, brute force would be inevitable. The moment they did, the network would respond. Lockdown. System hardening. Alerts sent to every known subnet—including Camellia's private guard. Everything Kenji had been building toward would vanish in a digital blink.

He made a decision.

He traced them back.

With a few keystrokes, he reversed their access trail—not to stop them.

To see who dared enter the lioness's den wearing borrowed paws.

His screen split. A trace route unspooled, leaping across servers, diving through proxies, peeling back layers of misdirection like bark from a dying tree.

And what he found at the root made his breath still.

He didn't type. He didn't speak.

He simply stared at the origin signature.

Then the corner of his mouth twitched.

"Of course it's you."

Elsewhere in the gallery, in a restricted control office framed with soft-glow monitors and locked glass doors, Vivianne's tablet buzzed in her palm. A subtle alert—one that had bypassed every standard firewall and landed in her private diagnostic layer. A breach.

She looked down. The source was buried deep. Very deep. Someone had threaded their way into the gallery's infrastructure—clean, surgical, but not perfect. They'd bypassed the visible security, yes. But not *all* of it.

Her eyes narrowed. "Not staff. Not external vendors. Not Camellia."

She activated a silent trace sequence, alerting the internal cybersecurity team through an encrypted relay. Her voice remained calm as she tapped her comm. "Initiate protocol blacklight. Immediate trace. Focus on any encrypted routing anomalies over the last fifteen minutes."

A voice returned in her earpiece. "Confirmed. One anomaly detected. Pattern consistent with cascade tracing. They're good."

"Not good enough. Peel them."

Lines of code bloomed across her screen, mirroring the uninvited presence as it tunneled closer to sensitive archives. Then—another anomaly. A second signal. This one quieter. Observing.

Vivianne's lips parted slightly. "You're watching too, aren't you? Whoever you are. Let's see who flinches first."

Minutes passed. Then a name surfaced—not exact, but close enough. One of the IP roots linked back to a shell company tied to Jules Devereux.

Vivianne stood still, eyes darkening like a storm tightening its spiral. "Of course."

The backtracking intensified. The gallery's system adapted—layers hardening, false data blooming like landmines. She wasn't just defending.

She was baiting.

The intruder responded. Brute protocols initiated. Alarms muted but ready.

Vivianne issued one more command, fingers still and deadly as a piano's final note. "If they push one layer deeper, bury the system. Lock them in with mirrors. Make them bleed."

The system's defense became a labyrinth of reflections, misdirected pathways, and malicious code masquerading as vulnerable data. The hacker took the bait—hook, line, and trace.

Vivianne's custom algorithm, disguised within the false archive files, infected their system with a data siphon. Within moments, she had access to their encrypted directories, exfiltrating fragments of operation codenames, shell company assets, and transaction logs buried beneath decades of digital camouflage.

Kenji, from his own node, watched silently.

He hadn't intervened when the bait was swallowed, nor when the virus sank its teeth in.

He simply tilted his head, amused.

Let them burn each other.

He had already slipped past the guards and into the temple.

Now it was only a matter of what relics he chose to steal.

Far from the gallery, across the Seine and down an alley disguised by morning mist, Alex emerged from a side entrance, his pace unhurried but uneasy. The air felt thick, unnatural. He glanced once behind him—habit—but the street was empty.

Until it wasn't.

A black van glided into view from nowhere, its engine barely audible. The back doors swung open. Before he could react, hands gripped him—trained, precise. A sharp prick in his neck, a sting of sedation. Gag. Blindfold. Bound wrists.

The van swallowed him whole.

Silence fell.

When Alex awoke, the world smelled of salt and rust. His vision cleared slowly—dim warehouse light filtering in from broken windows. His hands were bound to the arms of a steel chair. Across from him, lit like an oil painting in chiaroscuro light, sat Maris.

Not the Maris he remembered.

This one was draped in silk and danger, legs crossed, eyes unreadable.

Beside her: a table lined with instruments of delicate, deliberate purpose.

She smiled. Not kindly.

"You've missed your check-ins, Alex."

Her voice was honey over a blade.

"Let's fix that, shall we?"

Alex blinked against the low, flickering light, the sting of blood and sedative still buzzing in his veins. His wrists strained against leather straps—not coarse rope, but expensive, precise restraint. Every movement gave nothing but tension in return.

Across from him, Maris reclined in a sculptural metal chair, one leg elegantly crossed over the other. Her dress clung to her like smoke, satin catching the ambient light in bruised hues. She held a small silver object in her palm, idly rolling it between her fingers like a coin of judgment.

She didn't speak. Not yet.

Alex's throat worked. "Maris..."

Her eyes lifted, slow and unblinking. Predator's eyes in velvet shadow. "You forgot how to knock, Alex. Or how to report."

He opened his mouth to speak, but she lifted a finger—sharply. Silencing more than words.

"I don't want your apology. I want your clarity. Who are you loyal to?"

His breath hitched. "I never meant—"

Maris stood. The sound of her heels was softer than thunder but heavier than guilt. She moved to the table beside him, letting her fingers drift across the instruments—each one gleaming, deliberate, made for extraction. Of secrets. Of truth.

"You were sent to watch her. Not want her."

He closed his eyes. "It's not that simple."

She leaned in, breath like warm poison at his jaw. "It never is. But you don't get to fall in love with your subject, Alex. Not in this game. Not in mine."

His eyes opened—hollow, pleading.

And for a moment—just a breath caught between violence and vulnerability—something ancient and breaking passed between them.

"What am I supposed to do? Help me," he whispered.

Maris's voice slithered through the dark like a blade through silk: "Then start by bleeding. In truth. In detail. Tell me everything—"

Her mouth nearly brushed his ear.

"From the first time you laid eyes on her... to the moment you forgot you were never alone."

Maris snapped her fingers. Shadows moved.

Two figures emerged from the dark—masked, gloved, efficient. Maris didn't blink as they approached.

"Strip him."

Leather buckles gave way with slow deliberation. Alex struggled, instinct rising, but the sedative still pulsed in his bloodstream, muting resistance. His shirt was peeled away. Then his slacks. Skin met cold air. Exposure became ritual.

Maris stood unmoving as he was lifted from the chair. The figures carried him—delicately, deliberately—to a towering wheel at the far end of the room. It gleamed like ritual. Like judgment.

They affixed his wrists first, then ankles, spreading him into an X. The wheel turned slowly, locking in place. Naked. Bound. Offered.

Maris approached with the calm of a high priestess before sacrifice.

She touched his jaw, soft as a lover.

"Now," she said, voice like smoke curling around a blade. "Let's see what truths your body remembers before your tongue does."

From the tray next to him, she selected a slim syringe filled with a vivid violet serum—*Red Veil*, the compound known to ignite hyperarousal, overstimulate receptors, and fray the edge between agony and longing. Without warning, she injected it into the crook of his thigh.

Alex gasped.

Heat tore through his veins like liquid fever. Every inch of skin awakened, too aware, too alive. His breath hitched. Muscles trembled.

Maris trailed her fingers down his chest—soft, lingering, cruel.

"Breathe," she whispered, her tongue flicking just behind his ear. "This is only the beginning."

Next came *Devil's Thread*—a clear solution, deceptively pure. It amplified pain. Made a whisper feel like a scream. She injected it at the base of his ribs.

Alex cried out, low and guttural. His head jerked back. His eyes flared wide.

Maris circled him like a dark star, fingers grazing the underside of his jaw, the back of his knee, the hollow of his hip. Every brush left his nerves screaming. Begging.

She kissed the inside of his wrist—lightly—then bit just hard enough to make his spine arch.

"Still with me?" she cooed. "Good. I need your mind intact."

Then came the final vial.

Auraline.

The hallucinogen. Dreams twisted into nightmares. Lust shaped into visions.

She injected it at the base of his neck.

He didn't scream.

He moaned.

Eyes glassed, chest heaving, he sagged in the restraints as the compound laced through his mind like firelight through fog.

Maris stepped back, watching him burn beautifully in silence.

She whispered—not to him, but to the room.

"Now... let's hear the truth."

The world peeled back in layers.

At first, there was only sensation. The electric scream of nerves, the aching pull of desire coiled into something violent. His skin burned. Not like fire— but like memory. Everything was *too much.*

Red Veil lit every synapse like match-tips against wet skin. Devil's Thread carved whispers into shouts. And now—Auraline.

Auraline pulled the floor out from under him.

He saw Camellia's face—smiling. Then dissolving.

He felt Maris's breath—close, hot, sharp. But her eyes were nowhere. Her eyes were *everywhere.*

Alex tried to cling to anger. To purpose. But the chemicals stripped him bare. They didn't just expose—they excavated.

Still, something inside him snarled.

You are not theirs. You are not hers.

He clenched his fists, the straps biting into flesh. A whimper curled in his throat but never left.

He wouldn't give her the scream.

Maris leaned in, voice velvet and heat.

"You're shaking, Alex. Is that fear... or hunger?"

He bared his teeth. "Do your worst."

She smiled.

"Oh, darling. This *is* the foreplay."
And then the wheel turned again—slow, deliberate. Shadows danced.
And the unraveling began.

Chapter Nine: Before the Mirror Cracks

The digital storm had quieted. The lines of code that once pulsed with hostile intent now lay dormant, frozen trophies of a battle fought without sound. The glow of monitors faded into a cold blue hue, like the dying breath of a machine god. In the hush that followed, Vivianne stood alone in the sub-security suite buried beneath Galerie Solé, her silhouette outlined in the afterburn of code. Her fingers rested lightly on the matte surface of her tablet, the pulse at her neck a steady drumbeat of triumph and dread.

The main screen displayed cascading data extractions—names, accounts, shell corporations, bribes. And deeper: encrypted handoffs, illicit lab contracts, photos of vanished bodies and gilded lies. The digital trail bled red, unmistakably tainted by the signature rot of Jules Devereux.

She had done it.

No alarms. No footprints. Only results.

Vivianne exhaled through her nose, brushing a loose strand of hair behind her ear—not from vanity, but ritual. She straightened the hem of her tailored jacket, smoothed the creases born of long tension, and tapped the screen. The files locked with a coded signature only Camellia could break. The last line of encryption whispered into place like a breath behind a confession.

Then, like a dagger returned to its velvet sheath, she ascended the back stairwell, her steps soundless, her purpose sharp.

Camellia stood before the tall mirror in her penthouse study, porcelain mug cooling in her hands. Steam curled from it like the last exhale of a dying secret. The reflection in the mirror didn't move. It observed. Studied. Judged.

She had not slept. Not really. Not since the dossier arrived, heavy with ghosts and things left unsaid. Not since the shadows began to stretch longer in her gallery, brushing walls they had no business touching. Her reflection remained poised, dressed in stillness. But beneath the surface, something fractured whispered for release.

Vivianne entered without a word. The door sealed shut behind her like the clasp of a casket. She approached slowly and extended the encrypted drive with both hands—an offering without ceremony, but heavy with consequence.

Camellia took it without looking.

Only when the device clicked into its receiver did her voice cut the silence. "Tell me."

Vivianne clasped her hands behind her back, spine straight. "Three shell companies. All traceable to Devereux. One funds restoration efforts in Barcelona—cover for artifact laundering. The second's a Marrakesh-based front, pushing stolen antiquities through elite auctions. The third—"

"Paris?" Camellia's voice was flat, anticipatory.

Vivianne's mouth twitched. "Versailles."

Camellia's lips parted. Not in shock. In precision. Her thoughts clicked into alignment.

"What else?"

Vivianne lowered her voice, the timbre dark. "He holds the patent on a classified neurochemical compound. Synthesized covertly in a private lab posing as a neurological research institute in Geneva."

Camellia turned, slow and deliberate, her mug now forgotten.

"The same one?"

Vivianne nodded once. "Red Veil. Its progenitor."

The temperature in the room seemed to drop. Even the light dimmed, as though reluctant to touch the truth laid bare.

Camellia crossed the room and swept a hand across her desk. Data lit the space in ghostly projections—financial trails, chemical patents, confidential psychological research, all riddled with his fingerprints. Her gaze locked on a file labeled: *LAVALLIÈRE*.

Her voice, when it came, was more incantation than speech. "He used this to own them. Artists. Clients. Lovers. Their bodies. Their will."

Vivianne remained still. A blade in human shape.

"He's not untouchable," Camellia whispered. Not to Vivianne. To the reflection still watching in the mirror. "No man who traffics in ghosts ever is."

A pause, heavy and holy.

Then her voice, iron beneath silk:

"Prepare the gallery. He'll come for me next."

Vivianne's nod was slow, resolute. "And if he doesn't?"

Camellia turned to face the mirror again, her expression unreadable, half-shadowed.

"Then we drag him out by his reflection."

Elsewhere, beneath the skin of Paris in Montmartre...

The room stank of ozone and fear.

Jules Devereux stood in silence before his team, backlit by the eerie flicker of screens still catching their breath from failure. Around him, his top security analysts—men and women who had once been ghosts in the digital world—sweated under the weight of his gaze. No one dared speak first.

He let the silence rot.

When he finally stepped forward, his voice was almost gentle. "Tell me again. How did we lose access to something I *already* owned?"

The team lead, a wiry man named Severin, cleared his throat. "The gallery's system... had redundancies we hadn't anticipated. Adaptive learning code, mirror traps, malicious firewalls. We didn't expect a live trace from inside."

Jules raised one brow. The kind of movement that felt like a blade being unsheathed in the dark. "Didn't expect, or didn't prepare?"

Severin swallowed. "It was beyond projected countermeasures."

"*Projected.*" Jules whispered the word like a curse.

He began to walk, slow and unblinking, past their trembling bodies. The soles of his shoes echoed on the cement floor like a metronome marking the end.

"Do you know what projection is, Severin? It's an illusion wrapped in arrogance. A fantasy you wear like armor—until someone more clever finds the seams. And then?"

101

He stopped. Right in front of the team lead. Nose to nose.

"You bleed."

Severin flinched but held his ground.

Jules smiled—thin, predatory. "You failed. And now she knows I'm looking. Camellia Solé is not a woman who forgets footsteps in her gallery. She'll dig. She'll bite. She'll remember."

He turned, gaze sweeping the room. "Do you know what you've cost me? Leverage. Secrets. The silence of my enemies. I had them all. And now? They're emboldened. They're aware. All because you let a ghost out of her cage."

He opened a tall, polished cabinet mounted into the back wall. From within, he drew a black velvet-lined case.

Inside, a single weapon gleamed: a dueling pistol—antique, etched in obsidian scrollwork, but modified to fire .45 ACP.

Jules turned slowly, pistol in hand. "I have always believed in ceremony. In balance. In demonstration."

He cocked the hammer.

Severin's breath caught. "Sir—please, I—"

"You compromised my name. My reach. My legend. And you did so with your eyes wide open. That... deserves closure."

He didn't shout. Didn't flinch.

He pulled the trigger.

The sound was final. Brains and bone splattered the concrete. Severin's body crumpled, twitching once before stilling.

Blood pooled in silence.

Jules lowered the weapon and turned to the rest of the room.

"The next failure will not be theatrical. It will be intimate. And you will not see it coming."

He let the pistol rest against his side like an afterthought, then took a long breath, the only sound left in the room.

"Find me a new lead. Find me the source. Or find your replacement."

Then he walked away, the pistol still warm, his footsteps clean.

The silence he left behind begged to scream—but didn't dare.

Meanwhile at the warehouse in Île Seguin, drenched in shadow and salt...

Alex hung like a blasphemy against the wheel—naked, trembling, his breath dragged ragged between clenched teeth. Every nerve screamed. Every pulse of his heart echoed like thunder beneath his skin. The cocktail in his veins danced a mad ballet: Devil's Thread gnawed at every pain receptor, Red Veil dragged him toward the edge of arousal and madness, and Auraline blurred the lines between hallucination and memory until reality was little more than static.

His muscles twitched with phantom stimuli—kisses that weren't there, fingers that never touched, and voices that came from nowhere but felt like they belonged inside his bones.

He saw Camellia in flickers—smiling, then scolding. Maris too—lips parted, breath warm, hands that soothed and destroyed. They blurred. Became one. Became none.

And yet—beneath it all, Alex clung to something.

Maris watched him from a few paces away, arms crossed, eyes unreadable. She was no longer the soft shadow he once danced with. She was the steel beneath it. The consequence.

He shuddered violently.

She stepped forward.

"You're shaking," she murmured, dragging a gloved finger across his collarbone, watching his body flinch at even the featherlight contact. "But not from fear anymore."

He tried to speak. His throat scraped out a hoarse, "You don't have to do this."

Maris tilted her head. "I already am." She pressed her palm to his chest, feeling his heart trying to beat its way out. "You know what I admire most about you, Alex? Even like this—undone—you keep trying to lie with your eyes."

He looked at her then, truly looked—past the sculpted beauty and into the storm behind her gaze.

"You want me to hate you," he whispered. "But you're too careful. You still care."

A shadow passed through her features. Regret. Or rage. Or both.

She reached behind her and lifted a polished rod from the tray—cold steel, lacquered grip, tipped with a needle-thin sensor that shimmered faintly in the light. A feedback tool.

Alex tensed.

Maris leaned close, her breath on his lips like steam before a scream. "This isn't punishment," she said softly. "This is prevention."

Then she pressed the tool just below his ribs.

A pulse of electric sensation raced through him—pleasure folded inside pain, a scream choked by a moan. He bucked. The wheel rattled. His fingers clawed at the restraints.

"I can teach you the difference," Maris whispered, dragging the rod down his abdomen in a slow arc. "Between surrender... and obedience."

A tear slipped from the corner of his eye, not from pain, but from confusion. He was unraveling. And she was watching every thread fall.

Alex gasped, "What do you want from me?"

Maris touched her fingers to his jaw, tilting his head just enough so his eyes met hers.

"Everything," she said. "But first... I want your truth."

She leaned in. Her lips brushed his ear like a secret.

"Why did you fall for her?"

He didn't answer.

Not because he wouldn't.

But because in this moment, with his mind fractured by hallucinations, his flesh caught between torment and desire—

He didn't know.

Maris didn't speak right away. She circled him again, her heels echoing with the rhythm of judgment. The steel rod was returned to the tray with a soft clink. Her gloves whispered as she pulled them off, finger by finger, folding them over like secrets.

"You still think this is about control," she said, her voice low, as she brushed the back of her knuckles against his jaw. "But control is the beginning. The real question is—what do you *fear* when there's nothing left to hold onto?"

Alex's breath was erratic, his body pulled taut by the drugs and the hallucinations still spooling behind his eyes.

"Is it pain you fear?" she murmured, reaching for a vial of water and lifting it to his cracked lips, letting a single drop fall onto his tongue. "Or is it the truth you've buried beneath that beautiful mask you wear for Camellia?"

His body trembled.

"You crave her adoration," she continued, a fingertip now dragging slowly along the line of his thigh, tracing where truth lived in nerve endings. "But you fear her judgment more. You want her to see you as strong, incorruptible. But you're not, are you?"

"Stop," he whispered, voice cracked and raw.

Maris leaned in, her lips a breath from his temple. "Then tell me what you *are.*"

"I don't know anymore," he rasped.

"Yes, you do." Her voice was silk over nails. "You were sent to destroy her. And somewhere along the way, you wanted her to save you."

His eyes burned. He blinked, and saw her—Camellia—pulling him into the dark, into desire, into purpose. And beneath that—Maris. Not a rescuer. A reckoner.

"She made me feel like I mattered. Like the lies I told myself could be true if she looked at me long enough."

Maris studied him. Then, gently, she touched his chest again, right over his heart.

"Then this is where we begin. Not with lies. Not with pain. But with the truth you hid even from yourself."

Her hand moved down, resting just above his pelvis. "I'll take everything, Alex. I'll break you open, piece by piece, until there's no room left for guilt or doubt. Only what's real."

He met her eyes. There was no hate there. Only the terrifying beginnings of surrender.

"Good," she whispered.

Then she turned, selecting a new tool from the tray—something slimmer, needle-thin, glowing faintly with internal current. It pulsed with anticipation in her hand.

"Let's try again. Who else knows?"

She dragged the tip across his hipbone, slow and deliberate.

"Careful, Alex. The truth is already leaking out of you. Don't let it drown you."

He opened his mouth, trembling.

And the confessions began.

Elsewhere, hidden deep within the Galerie Solé's virtual spine...

Kenji Moriyama moved like smoke through code. Not just typing now—he conducted. Each keystroke was a command, a whisper, a scalpel edge cutting beneath the gallery's synthetic skin. Beneath Vivianne's fiery purge of Jules's hackers, Kenji had laid his nest. Not in defiance. Not in competition. But in a deeper purpose.

He had mapped the underlayers of Galerie Solé's architecture like a cartographer of secrets. Nodes. Pressure points. Behavioral learning loops. His cloaked presence slipped through mimic protocols and electromagnetic decoys, a digital revenant hidden in the wires.

The gallery's heartbeat thrummed around him.

He was still watching.

But not for Camellia's sake.

A soft chime broke the rhythm. The auxiliary screen to his right flickered blue. Encrypted call incoming.

Kenji tapped it open without hesitation.

The voice that came through was distorted, androgynous, layered in aural camouflage—but familiar in the marrow of his bones. His handler. The only voice that ever gave him orders.

"Report."

Kenji's eyes skimmed the active feed—dozens of frames in motion. One rendered Camellia's latest data extracts, highlighted files marked *LAVALLIERE*, *VEL SOLARIA*, and surveillance anomalies. Another tracked Vivianne's system patch logs. Another showed Maris—still, unreadable, coiled like a storm around a wheel-bound Alex.

"Vivianne neutralized Devereux's intrusion. Elegant, ruthless. She buried them beneath mirrored protocols and infected their stack with a custom siphon. Camellia now holds proof of three of Jules's laundering networks. One confirmed to house the precursor compound for Red Veil."

Silence stretched like tension wire.

"And Maris?"

Kenji hesitated. His fingers hovered above the console.

"She has Alex. Secured. Interrogation ongoing. The cocktail has taken effect. She's precise... meticulous."

"Is he alive?"

"Yes. For now."

"And Maris?"

Kenji's throat flexed. "She's not rogue... yet. But she's personal. She's digging deeper than protocol allows. This isn't extraction. It's... reclamation."

Another pause.

"And Camellia?"

Kenji's tone dropped. "Still unaware. But not for long. The tempo of her patterns are changing. She's about to connect the dots."

The voice on the other end hardened. "And Alex?"

"He's slipping. His mind is fragmenting. But the core of him... it's still resisting."

"That resistance is dangerous."

"It's also why he's valuable."

Static hummed for a moment, then the voice returned, flat and final:

"Prepare to intervene. If Jules makes contact with Camellia before we do, disrupt. Subtly if possible. Fatally if required. Containment first. Elimination second."

Kenji stared at the pulsing cursor. His fingers tapped a short confirmation: "Understood."

The call terminated.

Kenji leaned back into the shadows of the server alcove, breath quiet but shallow.

Elsewhere, in the underbelly of Montmartre, veiled by damp stone and candlelight...

Jules Devereux sat in a sunken chair of dark velvet, legs crossed, the antique pistol resting like a king's scepter across his lap. The air buzzed with the sting of ozone and the faint copper tang of blood not yet spilled.

Before him, Luciano stood like a silent wall of flesh and precision, his eyes cold, awaiting command. There were men who handled problems, and then there was Luciano "El Cazador" the kind of solution whispered before a body hit the floor.

Across the room, two surviving analysts from Severin's ruined operation knelt in silence, heads bowed—not in remorse, but in anticipation of violence.

Jules spoke without looking at them. "It was never about the gallery. Not truly. That place is a shrine to control. Camellia Solé curates power like most people hang paintings. But what I had... was leverage. Quiet ownership. Invisible touch."

He uncrossed his legs slowly, leaned forward. The pistol shifted.

"And now... someone has stolen the touch. My reach. My eyes. My secrets."

Luciano didn't move. He didn't have to.

Jules continued, voice smooth but flayed of patience. "Do you know what it costs to maintain silence in this world? How many bribes, how many falsified ledgers, how many buried lives? One packet trace. One infected node. One whisper in the wrong circuit... and everything I built? Up in smoke."

He finally turned toward Luciano. "One of Camellia's people gutted our system. They didn't just defend—they retaliated. Strategically. Psychologically. They wanted me to know it."

Luciano nodded. "The hacker?"

"Still in the network. Still moving. Still breathing."

A pause. The pistol was lifted, polished with his cuff like a gentleman brushing dust from silverware.

"I want them burned."

Luciano's head dipped in acknowledgment. "Consider it done."

Jules looked at the remaining analysts. "They saw how Severin died. But they haven't learned."

Then, to no one in particular: "Send someone they'll never see coming. Make it beautiful. Make it silent. But before they die—make sure they know why."

He turned to Luciano again, voice lowering with gravity.

"You have forty-eight hours. Bring me the hacker alive instead... I will kill them myself."

Luciano's nod was near imperceptible.

Jules stood.

His eyes landed on one of the remaining analysts—a woman trembling near the wall.

He smiled, slow and cold.

"If you fail," he said, voice soft as silk against a throat, "I won't be using bullets next time. I'll be using teeth."

He took a step closer to her. She didn't breathe.

"And then... I'll visit your daughter in Reims. She paints, doesn't she? Delicate little hands. I wonder how she'd manage with just one."

He turned away, leaving the silence to tremble in his wake.

And not a soul dared to move.

Above ground, the gallery had returned to its curated stillness.

But beneath the marble and masked civility, something shifted. The rules. The players. The stakes.

Camellia held the drive Vivianne delivered like a loaded promise. What lay inside it could ruin Devereux—if she moved carefully. If she moved first.

But something in her reflection had changed. The stillness no longer looked like control.

It looked like the calm before detonation.

And so, she did what only a Solé would do in the face of chaos.

She threw a party.

Not just any party.

A masquerade.

One designed to summon every ghost, every rival, every voyeur pretending to be a patron.

Because if she was going to burn—

She would do it in velvet and flame, before the world.

Chapter Ten: The Sister Returned

From the moment the gilded gates of Galerie Solé parted for the evening, Paris itself seemed to hush.

Outside, the world watched.

Inside, it was a fever dream of excess and precision.

Camellia Solé stood at the top of the grand staircase like a deity disguised in velvet. Her gown, a midnight shroud of crystal-laced black and onyx embroidery, clung to her like a whispered threat. A mask of lace and obsidian obscured the sharp lines of her face, leaving only her lips exposed—painted the deep red of dried blood and defiance. She did not descend. She simply existed, above it all, as the chandeliers dripped molten light over the most decadent gathering the city had seen in decades.

The Masque d'Exposition, as she had branded it, was an invitation-only descent into curated sensuality and whispered sin. Political darlings, tech moguls, heiresses, industrialists, and aristocrats masquerading as philanthropists all mingled beneath the temple of her control. Waitstaff moved like ghosts, champagne flutes glimmered, and behind every polished mask was an agenda.

The art was alive tonight.

Literally.

Nude muses posed across floating platforms—their bodies painted in surrealism and hunger, eyes trained in performative stillness. Their skin shimmered beneath precise lighting, each muscle a deliberate brushstroke, each breath a whisper of tension. One woman was suspended in silk like a blooming orchid in midair, her skin a swirling canvas of violet and gold, nipples gilded and glistening, her limbs bent in an impossible posture of surrender and command. Another pair of men, adorned in nothing but lust and ochre brushstrokes, sat entangled on a dais beneath an arch of smoke-plumed branches, their bodies locked in a pose that hinted at both agony and ecstasy. One kissed the hollow of the other's throat while fingers splayed across taut thighs, unmoving but urgent.

Elsewhere, a trio of women lay beneath a cascade of rose petals, entwined in an erotic tableau that felt both ancient and futuristic—their curves painted in metallic hues, each mouth parted in silent invitation. One rested her cheek on the belly of another, eyes closed in surrender, while the third dripped honey from her fingertips onto their skin, each drop catching the light like nectar from Eden. Their bodies were warm sculpture—living altars posed in breathless praise.

A golden boy with cherubic curls crouched nearby on a plinth, his body painted with serpentine runes, his cock wrapped in red silk, his tongue pressed reverently to a chalice held by a masked older woman—an intimate act frozen in eternity, radiating myth and vice.

A man, blindfolded and collared, knelt in still devotion at the foot of a marble pedestal, his body inked in mirrored eyes and ancient script. His breath rose and fell in time with the music—he was a living altar, his trembling devotion a prayer answered in voyeurism.

Two women posed in front of a fractured mirror, backs arched toward one another, their lips ghosting a kiss they would never deliver. Their bodies were coated in shards of silver leaf, cracked like porcelain, as if they were reflections that had clawed their way into flesh.

High above, a suspended duo—a man and woman painted in midnight constellations—rotated slowly in aerial silks, their limbs entwined like a slow celestial dance. Every inch of contact between them was a promise unfulfilled, erotic tension wound taut through the room like wire.

Eroticism had become an installation, and desire was the only language anyone seemed fluent in. Patrons wandered with masks askew and breath uneven, some mesmerized by the raw intimacy on display, others longing to become the canvas themselves.

Maris, cloaked in black like a shadow made flesh, lingered in the gallery's periphery. She tracked movement. She scanned faces. But mostly, she watched Camellia.

Only Kenji and Alex knew she was there.

Then, a ripple of intuition slid down her spine. A signal—subtle, wordless—passed from Kenji. A shift in the current.

Without a sound, Maris vanished.

She slipped away from the gallery and out the rear hall, where crimson velvet gave way to cold stone. Her boots kissed the floor silently as she moved through the servant's corridor and toward the outer wing. Her breath fogged slightly in the sudden chill of the exterior dock.

The rear security lights were dead.

Two guards—silent, sprawled in awkward stillness—confirmed the worst.

She flattened herself against the wall, drawing a slim blade from beneath her coat. Shadows moved near the loading bay—three figures, dressed in dark tactical gear, disabling the backup grid and slipping tools into a side panel.

They were precise. Efficient.

And they didn't belong.

Maris didn't hesitate.

She moved like a whisper in a cathedral, silent and sacred, a melody of violence set to a dancer's grace. Her body slipped through the dark like poured ink, every movement calculated, lethal, beautiful.

The first man turned too late.

Her blade whispered across fabric and found flesh—a gliding incision to the thigh, followed by a pirouette that brought her elbow crashing into his temple. He collapsed without a sound, the soft thud of his body muffled by the chill.

The second wheeled around, pistol half-raised, but she spun low beneath his line of sight, swept his legs, then surged upward—her knee crushing into his ribs. As he doubled, she caught his face in her hands, almost tender, before slamming his skull against the concrete wall.

The third had only begun to raise his comm.

Maris pivoted, fingers dancing to her thigh-holster. A breath. A flick. A needle-thin dart whistled through the air and kissed his throat.

He went slack mid-motion, falling backward in stunned silence.

She exhaled slowly. Stood over the bodies like a priestess at her altar.

With one precise click of her comm—coded and clear—she sent her signal to Kenji.

The dance was over.

Then she melted back into the dark corridor just as the sounds of the masquerade reached her ears again—laughter, music, and the ache of strings.

Alex, having returned to his role, moved like silk over stone—clean-shaven and flawlessly composed, the very picture of obedient charm. He wove through the upper echelon with trays of absinthe pearls and silver champagne, every motion precise, every glance purposeful. His uniform hugged his form with polished elegance, and beneath his mask, his lips were set in a polite smile that never reached his eyes.

He was no longer just a servant—he was a symbol of curated submission, an elegant illusion of control dancing in the center of a storm.

His eyes flicked between Maris and Kenji—quiet signals exchanged with the softest tilt of the head, a fractional linger of the gaze. It was a language of shadows and silence, one of loyalty and unspoken warning. Every step he took was calculated, reactive—an agent hiding behind the polish of performance. He served drinks with reverence and precision, but beneath the elegance was a tension coiled tight—a readiness, a restraint, an obedience earned, not inherited.

He was watching.

And waiting.

Vivianne monitored from a discreet corner, her tuxedo-cut suit impeccable, mask matte and unyielding. Her earpiece whispered, her focus unwavering.

And then...

Jules Devereux arrived.

He didn't glide in—he prowled. The crowd seemed to know instinctively to make space, like animals sensing a predator. He wore decadence like a blade: a silver mask etched in antique filigree, shoulders squared in a black suit that shimmered like oil, and a mouth curved in something that wasn't quite a smile. Behind him, Luciano moved like a rumor of violence, his gloved hands folded, his eyes flat and alert. Jules walked like he already owned the room. But tonight, the room didn't bend so easily.

He approached Camellia slowly, savoring the climb of each step as if it were a hunt. Stopping just beneath her, he looked up like a man gazing at a statue he wanted to defile.

"Mademoiselle Solé," he purred, his voice smooth as satin soaked in poison. "Your gallery never disappoints. I feel positively... aroused."

Camellia didn't flinch. Her smile was sculpted. "Then I've done my job."

Jules chuckled, low and bitter, glancing at the muses above. "Tell me, do they volunteer? Or do they simply forget they were ever anything else?"

Her eyes narrowed behind the lace. "Consent is a craft, Mr. Devereux. Like influence. Like rot. It thrives in silence."

He stepped in, close enough that only air and ego separated them. "And how long before silence gives way to screams?"

Camellia tilted her head, her lips curving. "That depends. How loud do you plan to be when it's your secrets bleeding on the walls?"

Luciano tensed, shifting subtly. The atmosphere folded tighter.

Jules leaned in, his breath winter-cold. "You've been digging."

Camellia's voice dropped. "And you've been bleeding. Quietly, I might add."

"You don't know the storm you've invited."

"On the contrary," she murmured, her gaze cutting. "I curated it."

He stood straighter then, but his smile had sharpened. "You're clever, Camellia. But clever women die slower. They suffer first."

Her eyes didn't blink. "Then make sure you're watching when I don't."

His laugh was a knife. He turned, gesturing subtly to Luciano, who nodded once. Somewhere, quietly and efficiently, a hunt had begun.

Meanwhile, inside the gallery, tucked near the bar and draped in shadows, one of Luciano's men pressed a finger to his earpiece and frowned.

"Bravo-Two, status check. Come in."

Only static.

He tried again, lower, tighter. "Bravo-Two, confirm breach status."

Still nothing.

Luciano glanced at him, sharp and subtle.

The man gave the faintest shake of his head. "Dead channel."

Luciano's eyes narrowed. "Sweep it. Quietly."

The man nodded and slipped off through a side door, just as the music swelled.

Outside, the second team arrived to investigate the silence. They found the first unit down. No blood. No sign of struggle.

Just absence.

They moved to exfil—too late.

Kenji's elite squad, shrouded in dark tacticals and guided by ghost-signals, descended from the rooftop like a silent wave of consequence.

The first intruder didn't even scream—he simply vanished beneath the force of a silenced takedown.

The others barely had time to turn.

Flash-comms scrambled. Muzzle flashes blinked into shadows. A blade whispered past one throat. Another fell backwards into silence, eyes wide.

In less than two minutes, Luciano's entire secondary unit had been eradicated—systematically, ruthlessly.

The vehicles were stripped, scanned, then driven off site in a choreographed sweep. Bodies were wrapped and vanished into the Seine's cold mouth via a back-exit tunnel only Kenji's network knew existed.

Inside, not a ripple reached the masquerade.

And just as the final shadow disappeared, the gallery doors whispered open.

Kenji stood silently near a tall black sculpture, his posture unreadable, his mask expressionless. He knew what was about to happen. He knew she was coming.

And then the air changed.

As the doors whispered open with a hush that turned heads like gravity, she entered without fanfare—but she needed none. She wore no mask, only a deep crimson gown that clung to her like spilled wine and a veil of translucent silk that shimmered like breath. Her presence was a painting that demanded reverence. Every step she took echoed like a secret being confessed.

She was art.

She was thunder before the rain.

She was Dhalia.

Kenji didn't blink. He watched her like a man standing on the edge of something holy and damned. He had known she would come. He had not warned Maris. Because some truths required silence to grow their roots.

She moved through the gallery like a storm rehearsed in stillness. Guests parted without realizing they had. Hands lifted glasses to lips and forgot to drink. Jules turned as she passed him.

"Enchanté," he said with a nod, his tone slick with admiration.

Dhalia smiled, slow and deliberate. "I rarely come to cities anymore. But for the right gallery…"

Their eyes held for a fraction longer than necessary.

She moved on.

Toward the stairs.

Toward Camellia.

Camellia remained still, her spine regal, her fingers curled on the banister. Something tugged at her chest—nostalgia or nausea, she couldn't tell. The woman approaching radiated a familiarity that gnawed at the edges of her instincts.

Dhalia stopped just a few paces away, lifted her chin slightly.

"Your gallery," she said, "is exquisite. The world could use more dangerous beauty."

Camellia's reply came measured. "And fewer dangerous strangers."

Dhalia smirked. "We're only strangers until we speak the same language."

Camellia narrowed her gaze but said nothing.

Dhalia dipped her head, a mocking curtsy. "Merci. For the invitation."

Then she turned, disappearing back into the masquerade like ink in water.

Camellia didn't follow.

But the chill she left behind stayed.

From her post near the south wing, Vivianne's fingers danced across the screen of her discreet tablet. A sudden, silent alert blinked red in the lower corner—minimal, easily missed. But not by her.

She tapped it.

Footage loaded—grainy, but clear enough. The hidden surveillance node embedded in the base of a sculpture near the back corridor had activated during the breach. Three figures. Neutralized in swift, brutal silence. But it didn't end there.

The feed continued. Audio kicked in—low, muffled, but distinct. The soft shuffle of boots, the click of comms, and then—gunfire. Muffled pops, like a string of firecrackers under a velvet curtain. Bodies moved in shadows. More figures appeared. Then more gunfire—precise, merciless. And then silence. Clean. Erased.

She paused the feed on the shadowy form that glided through them like a blade in velvet.

Unidentified. Masked. But efficient. Familiar.

Vivianne didn't flinch. She simply tucked the tablet away, stood straighter, and adjusted the line of her jacket. Then, with the ease of a ghost, she vanished into the flow of guests.

Later, once the last toast had been made and the guests had begun their elegant retreat, Camellia addressed the staff in the lower vestibule. Her mask was gone now, but the steel in her eyes remained.

"You were exceptional," she said. "As always."

The staff bowed in acknowledgment. The air was thick with relief and reverence.

As they turned to leave, Vivianne stepped forward and handed Camellia the tablet. Her voice was low, crisp.

"Footage. From the south sculpture feed. It caught everything."

Camellia took it, her thumb pressing against the screen. As the footage began to play, her expression didn't change.

But her silence was the promise of thunder.

"Dismiss them all," she said. "Except Alex."

Vivianne nodded once, then melted into the corridor to carry out the order.

Camellia remained where she stood, the tablet cradled in her hand, the images dancing across her eyes like ghosts from a war only she remembered.

Somewhere above, the chandeliers still flickered.

But in her mind, the gallery had already caught fire.

Chapter Eleven: Her Name

The last notes of music had long faded into the corners of Galerie Solé, leaving only the whisper of silk against marble and the muted shuffle of staff moving like ghosts through the aftermath. The masquerade was over, but the unease it birthed lingered, thick and metallic in the air.

Camellia stood beneath the last flickering chandelier, the weight of silence heavy on her shoulders. The tablet Vivianne had given her remained at her side like a weapon, its screen dark now—but the images still burned in her mind. The blurred figures. The precise violence. The crimson veil. The soundless storm that passed through her gallery as if she had summoned it.

And then the voice.

The voice that should have been ash and memory.

Camellia had not moved from her place since Dhalia disappeared into the crowd. The mask was gone. The gallery was nearly emptied. But the storm inside her had only just begun.

She descended the staircase slowly, each step a silent decree.

In the lower vestibule, her staff waited—still polished, still composed.

"You were exceptional," Camellia said, her voice low, controlled. No hint of falter, though her pulse screamed for it. "As always."

They bowed in unison.

Her tone sharpened. "Station guards at every exit. Double rotations tonight. No one leaves without my approval—not even vendors. We had an intrusion."

Vivianne stepped forward, crisp and unreadable.

Camellia turned to her, eyes like winter steel. "The woman in red. Find her. Guest logs. RSVP decrypts. Facial scans. Designer rentals. Every contact we've ever blackmailed—use them."

Vivianne's nod was exact. "Name?"

"I don't have one yet," Camellia replied. "But she knows mine."

Vivianne hesitated for only a breath, then vanished like a shadow that knew its orders.

The staff dispersed. The night shifted. Stillness crept back into the bones of the gallery.

Only Alex remained.

He didn't speak. He didn't offer comfort. He only watched—his presence steady, deferent, quiet.

Camellia turned to him, the elegant line of her spine rigid with something feral beneath the poise. Her gaze searched him—not for truth, but for silence. For obedience. For something she could touch without it slipping through her fingers.

"Come with me," she said.

It wasn't a request.

He followed.

They ascended the stairs in silence, marble and moonlight spilling around them. Her penthouse opened like a cathedral above the city, but tonight it felt like a crucible.

Inside, nothing felt still. The air vibrated. Gold light glowed across obsidian floors. Sculptures cast long shadows. And somewhere beneath the silence, Paris pulsed.

Camellia shed her coat first—slowly, deliberately. She let it slip from her shoulders to the floor without a glance. Then her gloves, peeled off finger by finger, placed on the tray beside the wine.

She moved like a woman in control.

But every step screamed.

Alex remained near the door, eyes following her like a predator taught not to bite. His hands were behind his back, but the tension in his frame betrayed the coil of want just beneath the surface.

Camellia poured herself a drink. Not wine this time, but brandy—something amber and old, something that burned.

She took a sip. Then turned to face him.

"You've been watching me all night," she said.

"I always watch you."

Her eyes narrowed slightly, but there was no real reprimand in her expression—only hunger. Not just for sex. For leverage. For stillness. For silence she could command.

"I don't need loyalty," she murmured, circling him now like a question. "I need obedience."

Alex's pulse ticked at his throat, but he didn't flinch. "Then show me where to kneel."

Camellia's lips parted—not in surprise, but in recognition. The offer was not new. But tonight, the stakes were different.

She reached for the buttons of his shirt, undoing them slowly—not to undress him, but to undress the moment. Her fingers grazed the skin of his chest with a featherlight precision, as if testing how much she could claim without breaking herself open.

"I'm not asking," she whispered.

"You never do."

Her hand slid down, palm flat against his sternum, pressing him back until he touched the wall behind him. Cool marble met heat. Her other hand caught his jaw.

"This isn't about desire," she said, mouth just inches from his. "It's about power."

Alex's breath hitched. "They're the same, with you."

Her lips brushed his—once. A threat. A taste. And then she moved away.

"Strip," she commanded softly.

Alex obeyed. Slowly. Beautifully.

As each layer fell away—first the jacket, then the shirt, the belt, the tailored slacks—Camellia remained still. Regal. Unmoved.

She sat perched at the edge of the velvet chaise like it was a throne of her own making, one leg elegantly crossed over the other, a half-finished brandy held between fingers that hadn't trembled once all night. Her eyes tracked him with an intensity that was neither hunger nor affection—it was appraisal.

Cold. Knowing. Intimate. The kind of gaze that unmade a man without laying a hand on him.

She watched the way his collarbone caught the gold spill of the chandelier, how the definition of his abdomen rose and fell with breath he tried to control. His arousal stood proud, uninhibited. He made no attempt to hide it.

But more telling than anything was the way he met her stare.

He didn't avert his eyes.

Didn't lower his gaze.

He offered himself to her gaze as an artifact of devotion, a body sculpted by uncertainty and need—but one that belonged, tonight, to her.

Camellia sipped the last of her drink and set the crystal glass on the table beside her. The faint chime as it touched the surface rang like a bell of judgment.

"Now come," she said, voice soft, measured. "But not to touch me."

He approached with reverent slowness, then knelt.

There was no hesitation.

Just stillness.

Obedience made flesh.

She uncrossed her legs in deliberate silence, silk parting like theater curtains at the breathless moment before a performance. Her dress slid higher, revealing the firm line of her thighs, the liquid warmth of her skin, the black lace edging of garters and secrets. One heel remained on. The other had been discarded with disinterest. It made her asymmetry deliberate—like a painting half-finished and therefore more powerful.

With two fingers beneath his chin, she lifted his face. His jaw tensed under her touch, but his eyes—those amber, flame-flicker eyes—never left hers.

"You want to serve," she whispered, her tone low, like velvet dragged across bare skin. "But tonight, you don't get to taste."

She leaned in, her breath grazing his cheek, her lips so close they stirred the fine hairs at his temple.

"You get to beg."

The words sank into him like hooks dipped in honey, and something in his posture shifted—not in defeat, but in surrender. A beautiful relinquishing.

Camellia sat back, her thighs parted, her gaze consuming him not as a man, but as a prayer answered by control.

And for the first time since the gallery fell quiet, since the crimson veil disappeared into the dark, she allowed herself breath.

Not from exhaustion.

But release.

She exhaled.

And the power she inhaled in its place was holy.

Alex knelt motionless, spine straight, thighs parted, hands resting palm-up on his knees like a sculpture of obedience. His breath was shallow, but steady—a man restraining not only desire, but devotion.

Camellia watched him for a moment longer, her fingertips idly tracing the rim of her glass. She didn't speak.

She didn't need to.

The silence between them thickened—no longer empty, but expectant. It curled around them like smoke from a sacred fire. She shifted slightly on the chaise, one knee rising just enough to reveal the full line of her thigh and the garter strap that clung to it like a vow.

"You kneel like a man who knows what he is," she murmured at last.

Alex's voice was low, careful. "Yours."

A slow smile touched her lips—not soft, not warm. Sharp. Possessive.

"That word has weight in my mouth," she said. "Say it again."

"Yours," he repeated, firmer now.

She leaned forward, her fingers brushing over his jaw, then down his throat. Her nails grazed skin—not to wound, but to mark. "And yet I still see restraint in you, Alex. Even like this. You want to please me, but you're afraid to give everything."

"I'm not afraid," he whispered.

"No?" Her brow arched as she stood, rising over him like a verdict. The hem of her gown slipped free of her legs, a waterfall of silk and control. "Then prove it."

She stepped around him slowly, one hand sliding through his dark curls, gripping just tight enough to claim without pulling. Her body heat passed over his bare back, a breath of temptation and denial.

"Put your hands behind you," she said.

He obeyed.

She moved closer—pressing her thigh lightly against his shoulder, the scent of jasmine and sin settling over him like a fog. Her fingers moved to her bodice, unhooking the silk with agonizing leisure, letting the fabric loosen but not fall.

Alex didn't move. He didn't dare.

Camellia let the dress slip halfway down, revealing one perfect breast framed by lace. Her nipple tightened in the air, flushed with anticipation. She touched it gently, eyes locked on him.

"You don't get to touch," she said. "But you'll watch."

And he did—devoutly.

Her hand continued lower, past the valley of her ribs, over the arch of her waist, resting at the top of her thigh. She dipped her fingers beneath the lace, slowly, sensually, until her breath hitched—just once.

She closed her eyes for a moment.

Not in pleasure, but in power.

When they opened again, she saw him—hard, breathless, trembling beneath his skin.

"Say it again," she commanded.

"Yours."

"Louder."

"Yours," he growled, every muscle tense with restraint.

She smiled then, stepping back just out of reach, her fingers still wet with her own desire. She raised them to his lips—not to offer, but to tempt. He leaned in instinctively, tongue flicking out—but she pulled away.

"Not yet," she whispered.

And then she turned, walking toward the bed—bare feet silent on marble, silk slipping from her shoulders like nightfall.

She looked back once, over her shoulder.

"Well?"

He stood.

He followed.

And the rest of the night belonged to the woman who took control not by force, but by permission never given.

The bedroom opened like a dream stitched in shadows and desire.

Walls of matte obsidian framed by gold-veined marble, sheer curtains dancing faintly from the evening breeze slipping through a cracked window. A low fire flickered in the hearth—more for effect than warmth—casting molten reflections across the velvet-draped bed that stretched like a stage.

Camellia crossed the threshold with the unhurried elegance of a woman born to command. She didn't look back to see if Alex followed—his silence behind her was answer enough. The soft thud of his bare feet on the marble kept time with her breath.

She stopped at the edge of the bed, letting her gown slip completely from her body. It pooled around her ankles like a defeated rival. She didn't hide. Her nudity wasn't vulnerability—it was declaration. Her skin gleamed in the firelight, warm-toned and sculpted, every curve deliberate, every inch an invitation written in a language only the willing could suffer to understand.

Alex stood at the threshold.

Still.

Staring.

Want tethered every muscle in his body like ropes pulled taut.

Camellia didn't beckon. She sat on the bed, back straight, thighs parted just enough to remind him what he couldn't take—yet. She leaned back onto her palms, tilting her chin as if offering herself to worship but not to touch.

"Get on your knees again," she said softly.

He obeyed.

She extended one leg slowly, resting her heel against his chest. The pressure was light but unyielding.

"You've pleased me tonight," she murmured. "But that doesn't mean you're free."

"I don't want to be," he said.

Her gaze flared. "Good."

She moved her foot upward, sliding it to his shoulder, then guiding him to the floor. She stood again and stepped around him, reaching for the drawer beside the bed. From it, she drew silk restraints—black, smooth, untouched.

She dangled them between her fingers.

"Crawl."

Alex's breath caught.

But he did as he was told.

Each movement forward was slow, deliberate—shoulders tense, thighs flexing. He kept his eyes on the floor until he was at her feet, kneeling once again. She circled him like a patient sculptor, brushing the silk across his shoulder, his back, his jaw.

"Hands behind," she said.

He crossed his wrists without hesitation.

With measured care, she bound him.

Not tightly. Not painfully. But securely—intimately. A symbol. A contract.

When she finished, she stood before him again, bare and regal, the firelight licking the undersides of her breasts, casting her face in gold and shadow.

"Look at me."

He did.

And in that moment—tied, kneeling, eyes full of devotion and want—he had never looked more free.

Camellia stepped closer, straddling him slowly, her thighs brushing his hips, her hands cradling his jaw. She didn't kiss him. She didn't need to.

"You don't get to beg," she said, her voice a breath on his lips. "Not yet."

Her body pressed against his, not for pleasure, but to let him feel the heat he was denied.

"To beg," she whispered, "you must first be broken."

She rocked against him, just once, just enough to make him shudder. Then she rose, dragging her nails down his chest as she returned to the bed.

She lay back.

Sprawled.

Commanding.

A vision of consequence.

And she smiled.

"Now, Alex... let's see how long you last without your hands."

Alex's breath moved in shallow waves—controlled, reverent. The silk around his wrists held firm, a quiet hum of tension pulling across his back as he knelt beneath her gaze. The fire cracked once, casting fractured light across her skin. On the bed, Camellia looked like temptation sculpted from dusk—bare, poised, and utterly unyielding.

She parted her thighs, just enough to be generous. Not enough to be kind.

"Crawl to me," she said.

And he did—slowly, like a man who feared not punishment, but disappointing the god he worshipped.

Each movement toward her was a surrender. Each inch a prayer.

When he reached the edge of the bed, Camellia extended her leg and rested her foot against his shoulder. "Still," she murmured.

Alex froze.

She trailed her foot slowly along his collarbone, then across his throat. Her touch was delicate, but her stare was carved from flint.

"I want to see how much restraint lives in you," she whispered. "How deep your obedience runs."

He nodded, lips parting slightly.

Camellia tilted her hips forward, her fingers grazing down her own torso in full view. She drew a line between her breasts, over her navel, and lower, until her hand dipped beneath the shadow of her thigh. Not for him. For herself.

Alex's jaw clenched.

She watched him—watched the flicker of hunger wrestle with the worship in his eyes. "Does it ache?" she asked softly, circling herself with a measured stroke. "To kneel. To watch. To *not* be permitted?"

He swallowed, hard. "Yes."

"Good," she breathed, not slowing. "I want your ache. I want your silence."

She arched slightly, lips parting as her fingers moved with slow precision, her breath catching just enough to curl the edges of his restraint into agony.

"Speak," she commanded. "But only truth."

Alex's voice was low, ragged. "You're the only thing I want. The only name

I remember when I close my eyes."

Camellia's fingers stilled.

For just a moment.

Then she withdrew them and lifted her fingers to his lips.

"Open."

He did.

She placed them gently on his tongue, letting him taste the heat she'd denied him, the salt and silk of her control. His moan was soft—devout.

"You may watch me," she said, sliding back into the pillows, parting herself again. "But you may not touch."

Alex's body shook with restraint, the silk biting just slightly into his wrists. He knelt at the foot of her bed like a penitent knight, eyes fixed on her every motion.

She began again—slower now, more deliberate—never breaking eye contact.

She brought herself to the edge once... twice... never finishing, only sharpening the tension. Each time she paused, her breath caught, her body arched, and she whispered his name—not as invitation, but as command. As claim.

"Alex."

"Yes," he breathed.

"If I let you touch me..." Her voice curled like smoke. "Would you worship or consume?"

His jaw flexed. "Both."

She smiled then—dangerous, dark. "Then you'll have to earn the chance to try."

And finally, she slid forward, pulling him up with the slightest gesture.

She pressed his face between her thighs, close but not close enough.

"Breathe me in," she whispered. "But don't move until I say."

He shuddered. The scent of her, the heat—his body trembled with the effort of stillness.

She held him there, her hand resting gently on his head. Not pushing. Just *owning*.

"Now," she whispered, voice a blade wrapped in silk.

And when he moved, it wasn't with hunger.

It was with *devotion.*

She cried out—not because he was skilled, though he was. Not because he was eager, though he had always been.

But because for one single moment, as his mouth obeyed her every command, as her fingers gripped his hair and her thighs wrapped around the silence, Camellia no longer felt haunted.

She felt *whole.*

And as she shattered against him—body arching, cry choked into velvet— her exhale was not surrender.

It was *victory.*

The aftermath was not silence.

It was breath. Shallow, laced with unspeakable weight.

Camellia reclined against the obsidian headboard, silk sheets pooling around her hips like shadows returning to their master. One hand curled against her chest, the other slack at her side—fingers still curved as if they remembered the line of his jaw.

Alex knelt at the foot of the bed, naked and reverent, his chest rising with the steady rhythm of one who had worshipped without question. A sheen of sweat kissed his collarbones, and the silk she'd bound him with earlier left faint marks he did not hide.

Camellia stared upward, expression unreadable, gaze fixed on the ceiling like she was retracing constellations only she could decipher.

Not pleasure. Not affection.

Control.

Reclaimed through dominance. Tempered in restraint.

But now, the storm within her—contained by the act—began to move again.

She rose with practiced grace, posture immaculate, skin glowing in the gold cast of bedside light.

"That's enough," she said, voice calm and distant. Not dismissive. Conclusive.

Alex dressed in silence. When he glanced at her, it was without presumption.

Only reverence.

Camellia stood, poured another glass of brandy, and sipped.

"You may go."

She didn't look at him.

A pause.

"And tell no one what I gave you."

Alex adjusted the collar of his shirt, nodded once. "Of course, Mademoiselle Solé."

The door whispered closed behind him.

Camellia turned back toward the window, her reflection framed against the darkened Paris skyline. Below the surface of her breathless calm, calculation resumed its slow, predatory march.

The figure in red. The surveillance footage. That voice.

She hadn't said her name.

She didn't need to.

Who was this woman?

Camellia downed the rest of her drink, fingers tightening around the stem of the glass.

The night wasn't over.

One floor below, Alex moved like nothing had happened. The corridors were dim, the scent of sandalwood and champagne trailing in his wake.

Out the side entrance and into the cool hush of the alley. Paris was quieter here—honest, breathing in shadows.

He pulled the burner from his coat pocket. Three rings.

"Go." Maris's voice. Sharp. Measured.

"I'm out," Alex said. "The spiral's begun. She's slipping."

A pause.

"How far?"

He lit a cigarette, exhaled. "Far enough that she forgot herself. Not far enough to forget the ghost."

"Did she say the name?"

"No. But she bled it."

Kenji's voice, low in the background: "Was she compromised?"

"She's reinforced her defenses. Doubled staff. Locked every access point. She knows someone's inside."

"Status?" Maris asked.

Alex took another drag. "Used. Not broken. Close."

Kenji again: "Then we continue. Phase two. Stay embedded."

"She's in my head," Alex muttered. "She gets in the blood."

"That's the point," Maris said.

The call ended without ceremony.

Above, Galerie Solé loomed—sacred and haunted, its curator cracked and watching.

And below, in the hush where secrets breed, Alex walked deeper into the dark.

Chapter Twelve: Untouched, Untethered

The echo of Camellia's command still lingered in the gallery's bones.

The last of the gallery lights dimmed, but the echo of what transpired still pulsed through its marble bones. Camellia's scent lingered in the penthouse air—jasmine, brandy, and power. But beneath it all, there was something older now. Something broken open. The name she did not say had taken root in silence.

Vivianne stood alone in the archive corridor beneath Galerie Solé, the tablet cold in her hands.

The footage looped again—three figures breaching from the alley behind the gallery perimeter. They moved with silent efficiency. Fourteen seconds. One hadn't even drawn breath for a scream. Vivianne froze the frame, scanning every blurred angle: body weight distribution, strike patterns, heat signatures. These weren't drunk party crashers. These were professionals. Mercenaries.

She set a second file to render in the background—another angle from a discarded hallway cam she'd recovered before staff cleanup. It caught the same breach, but this time with sound. Not much—muffled thuds, one rapid-fire breath, a sharp intake.

No chatter.

No error.

Her fingers danced across the interface, isolating one blurry profile with a half-visible patch on the collar. She enhanced it three times before the fragment resolved—an insignia she recognized. But not from police logs. This one came from her previous life.

Black ops. Contracted. Global clearance, local deniability.

She blinked once, then began cross-referencing the insignia with her encrypted dossier of unofficial military contractors. It took ten minutes for the link to register and populate data fields with names. One name stood out the most—not a soldier, but a patron.

Jules Devereux.

Vivianne's stomach tightened.

She flagged the file and secured it in a private vault partition—Camellia would see it when Vivianne was sure.

But this was only half of what she had been tasked with.

With a sharp breath, Vivianne returned to the other task: the woman in red.

The footage from the ballroom stuttered, the pixelation from the mirrored columns casting glare across the screen. Still, she slowed the frame. There—the crimson silk again. A flash of a gloved hand brushing Camellia's arm. Not a grab. A message.

She zoomed in, adjusted luminance, inverted contrast. No face. The crimson veil she wore scattered light and disrupted facial recognition—engineered not just for beauty, but for anonymity.

But the posture—shoulders back, chin lowered ever so slightly—spoke volumes.

Vivianne paused, closed her eyes, and let memory do the sorting. She had catalogued posture signatures for counter-intelligence contracts. What stuck wasn't the stance itself—but the restraint. No wasted movement. No borrowed identity. Whoever she was, this woman had trained to vanish.

And she had.

No guest list entry. No cross-match on fashion rentals. No heat signature upon departure. Even the residual garment trace—tiny fibers she had collected from the plinth—revealed nothing unique.

Clean.

Sterile.

Professionally so.

Vivianne clenched her jaw. This wasn't evasion. This was omission. Someone had scrubbed this woman from the record entirely.

Not missed.

Removed.

She locked the footage, then retrieved a slim folder from a drawer—one of Camellia's red-tier contingency books. No matches. No possibilities.

Only gaps.

Vivianne opened her encrypted comm and typed:

TWO UNKNOWNS. FIRST TRACE: MERCENARY AFFILIATION CON-FIRMED. CLIENT LINKED TO DEVEREUX.

SECOND: NO DATA. INITIATING SECONDARY ALGORITHM.

She paused, hesitating only once before sending an additional line:

RECOMMEND PROVISIONAL SHADOW STATUS: GHOST.

She wouldn't bring Camellia half a trail.

Not yet.

But something was hunting.

And Vivianne—methodical, calculating, rarely afraid—felt the chill of it in her bones.

The woman in red hadn't come for the art.

She had come to be *seen*.

Deep underneath the city, a Black Site – Undisclosed Location

The walls were black. Not matte, not glass. Black like ink suspended in air—suffocating, without texture, without edge. A chamber without time.

Alex sat with his hands resting on his thighs, spine straight. No restraints. None were needed. He had arrived of his own will.

Maris stood in the corner of the room, partially backlit by a dim strip of artificial amber. The glow brushed the high arc of her cheekbones, the line of her throat. In this place, she did not speak first. She watched.

"Report," she said, at last.

Alex exhaled, slowly. "Camellia dismissed the others and called me back. Her voice didn't tremble, but her body language... shifted. Like she'd just seen something she couldn't control."

Maris stepped forward. The heels of her boots made no sound on the polished floor. "Before she summoned you—what did you observe?"

"She stood at the top of the stairs too long after the crowd thinned. The way she scanned the floor—it wasn't performance. She was tracking. Internally. Then she gave orders. Precision orders. Doubling security, locking the gallery perimeter, quarantining the vendor staff."

Maris lifted an eyebrow. "Any emotional leakage?"

Alex nodded, once. "When she looked at Vivianne—there was a crack. Barely perceptible, but real. She saw something... or someone. And it frightened her."

"The woman in red," Maris said, not as a question.

Alex didn't answer immediately. He rubbed his wrist as if the silk was still there. "She didn't say, but it was written into every movement that followed."

Maris's gaze darkened. "And with you?"

"She used me," he said plainly. "Not for comfort. For recalibration. She needed a fulcrum to reassert control."

"Did she break?" Kenji's voice, calm and quiet, filtered in from the surveillance terminal.

Alex shook his head. "She fragmented. But no, not broken. If anything, she's more dangerous now—because she remembers what fear feels like."

Maris folded her arms. "Did she mention the woman in red?"

"No," Alex said. "But she knew. It was in her eyes—every time I moved too close, every time I didn't flinch. Like she was comparing us. Measuring."

Kenji again, his tone low. "Did she say anything you didn't expect?"

Alex looked up. His voice was flat, but his eyes burned. "She said, 'Tell no one what I gave you.'"

A pause.

Maris stepped closer, her tone no longer just professional—curious. "And what did she give you?"

Alex didn't flinch. "Permission. To kneel. To worship. To want."

"And what did you give her?" Maris asked softly.

He hesitated.

"A taste," he said.

Silence hung. Kenji leaned in toward the console, adjusting something just out of view.

Maris's voice broke the quiet. "Then she's predictable. Still using intimacy as leverage. Still mistaking devotion for control."

Alex's mouth twisted, not quite into a smile. "No. She knew I would report back. That's what makes her dangerous."

Maris studied him then—truly studied him. "Are you still loyal?"

Alex didn't blink. "Yes."

"To whom?"

He met her eyes now.

"To the outcome."

Kenji nodded once. Maris turned away. The room exhaled with her.

"Good," she said. "Because what comes next will require you to mean it."

She left without another word, her figure vanishing into the dark like a memory receding.

Alex remained seated, eyes half-lidded, pulse steady.

Above them, Île Seguin shimmered in a different kind of silence.

And below it all, the war between sisters had begun again.

Meanwhile at the Devereux Estate – Subterranean Vault Room

The room was carved from imported Italian marble and cruelty. Every angle was exact, every light engineered for intimidation—not comfort. The chandelier above was black steel and frost-glass, casting fractured light across antique weaponry and velvet-bound ledgers of blood-soaked contracts.

Jules Devereux stood at the far end of the vault, hands braced on a lacquered table inlaid with old maps and newly updated kill lists.

He did not speak immediately.

He waited.

Luciano Navarro stood in still shadow across from him, tailored black suit pristine, leather gloves flexing once as if they'd grown restless. One boot angled forward, ready for the command that hadn't yet come.

Devereux finally moved.

He poured two fingers of something older than memory into cut crystal. He didn't offer it. He didn't need to.

The glass cracked as he set it down—slowly.

His voice, when it came, was cold velvet. "Two full teams. Nine men. Hardened. Trained. Gone."

Luciano said nothing.

"No comms. No fallback. No screams. Just... erased."

Devereux began to pace. Each step a heartbeat of controlled fury. "And Galerie Solé?" His tone sharpened. "Untouched. Camellia Solé? Still breathing. Still defiant."

Luciano inclined his head once. "The first team was eliminated behind the gallery. The second never made it past the eastern service corridor."

"Eliminated," Devereux echoed. "Not repelled. Not cornered. Taken out without hesitation."

"They weren't spared," Luciano said. "They were discarded."

Devereux's laugh came like a blade against glass. "So no message. No mercy. Just efficiency."

Luciano's tone was flat. "Indiscriminate. Precise."

Devereux exhaled through his nose, gaze swinging to the grainy footage flickering across the vault's embedded monitor. There she was—crimson silk, obsidian veil, gloved hand brushing past the chaos like a memory that refused to fade.

"And this one?" he asked, voice lowering to something softer. "The woman in red?"

Luciano's eyes followed the frozen frame. "She wasn't touched. Wasn't looked at. She moved as if nothing touched her could live."

Devereux said nothing for a long time.

Then—softly, hungrily: "She moved like prophecy."

He stepped closer to the screen, fingertips grazing the image without contact.

"She didn't flinch. She didn't run. She wanted to be seen. A flame dipped in silk and audacity."

He smiled—genuine this time. Reverent.

"She's not part of the chaos. She's something... *other*. A rare pulse from another world. Something art forgot how to birth."

Luciano remained silent.

Devereux turned back toward the bar and poured another drink—slower now, almost indulgent.

"She's not Camellia. She's older. Rarer. A collector's piece. A myth with breath and direction. I don't want her destroyed, Luciano."

He took a sip.

"I want her found. Tracked. And brought to me—*perfect*. No force. No violence. The smoothest of hands only. Like acquiring an antique fresco no one knows exists."

Luciano's brows knit faintly. "You don't think she's connected?"

Devereux waved a hand. "No. The blade that took out my men wasn't hers. She's untouched by that filth. She came for mystery, not carnage."

Luciano's voice was even. "Then there's a third player."

Devereux's smile vanished. "Yes. One who erases."

He stepped close to Luciano now.

"I want them found. All of them. The one who killed my men. The hacker still swimming through my vault's veins. *But not her*," he added, nodding to the screen. "She is to be handled with care. With taste."

Luciano's eyes narrowed. "The digital breach—we traced a proxy node to Amsterdam. Female patterning likely. Rotating locations. Could be hired. Could be personal."

Devereux slammed the glass down—this time it didn't crack.

"She breached *me*. Not Camellia. Not the gallery. *Me*."

He moved fast—three strides forward—until he was face to face with Luciano.

"Do you know what it means when my name becomes accessible? It means I am not feared enough."

Luciano didn't move. "Then let me correct it."

Devereux leaned in, breath quiet, deadly. "And if they're all connected? The hacker, the phantom blade?"

Luciano's voice dropped. "Then I'll string them up in sequence—hacker, shadow, asset. And I'll gift you their truths before their hearts stop beating."

Devereux smiled—slow, sensuous, unholy.

"No. Not the woman in red."

He brushed invisible dust from his cuff.

"She's not a threat. She's a possibility. And I intend to possess her."

He turned toward the massive vault doors and gave the softest of commands.

"El Cazador hunts."

Luciano nodded once and left like a storm sealed in skin.

When the doors slammed shut, Devereux finally allowed the glass to break in his hand.

Not from rage.

From anticipation.

Chapter Thirteen: Obedience in Red

Paris exhaled beneath a shroud of whispers. Somewhere above the Seine, the moon fractured in the ripples of black water, its reflection trembling just enough to suggest unrest. Power shifted in shadows before it ever did in headlines—and tonight, the current had changed direction.

Kenji Moriyama walked like a man who belonged nowhere.

Kenji didn't take the direct route. He never did—not out of paranoia, but ritual. It was a dance of disappearance, not evasion. Three transfers across metro lines, each with a change in gait, expression, and posture. A café window reflection became a rearview mirror. An abandoned storefront became a moment of stillness. A man with a folded newspaper in one hand and nothing in the other.

By the time he surfaced from the final underpass, his silhouette had altered. His suit—tailored, quiet, immaculate—no longer said "agent." It said accountant if read too quickly. Diplomat if watched too long. His gloves stayed on.

The meeting place was beneath a defunct language institute in the 15th arrondissement, two blocks from a shuttered theater and a wine cellar no one remembered owning.

He entered through the alley gate that hadn't creaked in decades. The key wasn't metal—it was cadence. A sequence of four knocks, then silence. Then two more, like breath returning after absence.

The door opened. No words were exchanged. Kenji descended.

The descent opened into a chamber that hummed with silence. No decoration adorned the walls—just industrial concrete softened only by the burnished gleam of polished floors and the symmetrical alignment of bodies on either side. Twelve operatives—six on each flank—stood in identical posture, heads bowed, arms behind their backs. Their suits varied in shade, but not in severity. Masks were not worn here. Trust was too dear, and failure too final.

Kenji stepped onto the dark line running down the center of the room. He walked between them like a current through wire—silent, inevitable, live. No one moved. No one spoke.

At the far end stood the figure who had summoned him. Kenji's handler. Their back was to him, posture relaxed in the way only absolute control allows. The room might've held breath—if any dared. Kenji reached the end of the path and stopped exactly one meter behind the figure. He bowed—not deeply, but precisely. He waited.

The room was warm with stillness. Not heat—intention. A captive. A survivor from the masquerade onslaught sat restrained but upright, breath shallow, pulse betraying the veneer of control he tried to maintain. Sweat traced the hollow of his throat, pooling beneath his collar. The handler stood a few feet away, back still turned. Then—movement. Slow. Deliberate.

Black gloves lifted a smooth ceramic mask from the desk beside them— white porcelain, high-cheeked, blank save for the faintest trace of red at the mouth. They held it like something sacred, or damning. Kenji didn't blink as the mask was drawn over the handler's face and secured with a whisper of ribbon.

Only once the mask was in place did the handler speak. "Begin the descent."

A low hum answered as a near-invisible scarlet vapor curled from the inset nozzles near the captive's chair. Auraline. Not injected. Inhaled.

The man's eyes flicked wide—then blinked. His jaw slackened. Breath caught in his throat. A pause. Then came the first hallucination. He saw lips—lush, painted, just shy of touching his. He felt the press of silk against his neck. He inhaled—and it smelled like skin warmed by candlelight and danger.

The handler stepped forward, voice coated in velvet. "Tell me your name."

A shiver passed through him. His lips parted, as if remembering how to speak. "Mathis... Vorel."

The handler circled—slow, predatory. Every step was a question. Every silence was permission to yield.

"Who do you work for?"

Mathis's chest rose, fell. He saw fingertips brushing his jaw. A breath at his ear. He swallowed a whimper and whispered, "Jules... Devereux..."

The handler didn't press. Just stood close enough for the hallucinations to deepen. Auraline was not about pain—it was seduction of the mind's defenses.

"What was your purpose at the Masquerade?"

Mathis exhaled hard, like arousal had become confession. "Diversion... Team One was meant to breach the service corridor. Team Two—plant surveillance nodes. Camellia was the target. Alive. Shaken. Not... harmed."

"Who sent you?"

The hallucination shifted—he was naked beneath layers of red silk. Each answer he gave peeled it back. He didn't want to stop. "Devereux gave the primary order..."

Another beat. "But..."

The handler leaned in, saying nothing.

Mathis moaned.

"There's a woman..." he rasped, pupils wide, glistening as the Auraline took deeper root. "I don't know her name. No one does. She appeared once... at the masquerade. Red silk. Veil like smoke."

"She walked past death like it belonged to her. Didn't speak to anyone... except Camellia. Just for a moment. But it was enough."

The handler tilted her head—delicate. Curious. Dangerous.

Mathis gasped. "She wore gloves... white. Not for warmth. For distance."

"Devereux talks about her like... like she's art. Like he saw God and wanted to hang her in a private wing."

"He said she moved like prophecy. Like a dream so sharp it leaves scars."

"He doesn't know who she is... but he wants her. Not to kill. To possess."

The handler took a slow step forward.

"He called her... a relic with breath. A whisper no man should raise his voice around."

142

"She didn't say much. No one heard her. Just that one moment with Camellia. But it changed everything."

"She touched Camellia's arm... and smiled. No one smiles like that unless they mean to undo you."

"Devereux doesn't want to conquer her. He wants to kneel."

The handler remained still. But beneath the mask, her smirk curved slowly—pleasure blooming like poison in full flower.

"And what do you know about the hacker?"

The handler's voice was silk scraped across metal—soft, but with edges.

Mathis gasped. "I don't know who it is. But... the signature—it's old. Government-old. Pre-dissolution protocol. They're ghostwalking through dead networks. Female-patterned."

"She's not just a hacker. She's a revenant. Using extinct code."

"Motivation?"

"Not money... not power... It started with Jules. He ordered the breach—wanted everything. Records. Accounts. Proof to bury Camellia. Take her down. Strip her name. Own what she built."

"But the gallery didn't lock him out."

"It welcomed the touch... just long enough."

"She followed it back. Slid into his vaults. No force. No noise. Just... precision."

"She didn't steal. She observed. Altered a few things. Left behind a... signal."

"She didn't just retaliate... she made it art."

"She wasn't just protecting Camellia... she was after something else. Like a command whispered through code."

"She's not chasing truth. She knows it."

"She doesn't want to take him down... she wants to unmake him."

The handler stepped back slowly.

"Devereux wants her. Not like the woman in red. He doesn't want to possess this one. He wants to break her. Himself."

"He said she made him visible. That she touched his name in the dark."

"And now... he wants to erase her."

The moan faded. Mathis slumped in the chair—trembling, emptied of secrets.

The handler stood still. Porcelain mask in place.

Kenji stepped forward from the shadows.

"Sedate him."

Kenji nodded. A second operative emerged with a syringe.

"Everything after the masquerade," the handler continued. "Scrub it. Layer false echoes. Panic. Chaos. A raid gone wrong."

"Make him forget her voice," she added. "But leave the ache."

Kenji raised an eyebrow. "A scar?"

"A craving," she said. "Let Jules feel the weight of missing something he never owned."

As Mathis faded beneath the sedative, the handler turned and exited.

Kenji followed.

The private chamber waited. Velvet walls, antique table, silence.

The mask came off.

Dhalia Solé. Alive.

Her eyes—obsidian. Her presence—unholy.

Kenji closed the door.

"Well?" she asked.

"We got what we needed. Mathis will remember nothing useful."

"Vivianne?"

"She moved efficiently. Camellia gave full authority."

Dhalia smiled faintly. "Of course she did."

"Devereux is bleeding," she said. "He doesn't even know where."

"She will respond," Kenji said.

"Let her."

"She needs the chaos." She leaned in. "And who lives at the center, Kenji?"

He said nothing.

"Me."

Dhalia turned to a panel. A drawer hissed open. The crimson veil waited.

"She saw me once," she said. "That's all it takes."

"Dump him."

Kenji inclined his head.

"No message. No marks. Leave him on the Devereux estate steps. Still warm. Still sedated. Nothing in his mind but a whiff of smoke and fear."

"No witnesses. No trace."

"Let Jules wonder what it cost me to spare him."

Kenji tilted his head and smirked. Then, gently— "のは What's your next move, Dhalia?"

Dhalia's smile curved like silk drawn over a dagger.

Kenji paused at the threshold, his eyes steady on her silhouette.

Dhalia turned slightly, just enough for her eyes to meet his.

"I plan to set the trap..." she said. "And be the bait."

She leaned closer, breath warm with certainty. "He doesn't want a war. He wants worship. I'll give him just enough divinity to drown in."

Kenji's smirk was brief but real. Then he bowed.

Just before he vanished through the velvet corridor, her voice followed. "をつけてね... Kenji." [Take care, Kenji.]

Dhalia stood alone. Mask off. Gloves off. Veil untouched.

The war had begun.

Chapter Fourteen: The Anatomy of Want

The silence left behind by Kenji's departure was not emptiness—it was orchestration. Like the breath held before a symphony's first strike, it lingered with intent. Dhalia remained motionless, letting the quiet settle over her like ash. The veil still rested untouched beside her, but now the air had changed. It wasn't aftermath. It was ignition.

Her fingers hovered once more over the crimson veil, then withdrew. Not yet.

Instead, she turned toward the panel behind her and pressed her bare palm to it. A quiet chime acknowledged the request. A moment later, a discreet door hissed open across the room.

An attendant stepped in—young, sharp-eyed, and dressed in grayscale uniform without insignia. She bowed deeply but didn't speak. Names weren't exchanged in this space. Dhalia preferred it that way. Intimacy without familiarity. Precision without contamination.

"Begin surveillance preparations," Dhalia said, her voice low and clear. "Begin cataloging every café, restaurant, and event venue Devereux frequents—past and present," Dhalia said, not turning to face her. "Start with his haunts in the 1st and 8th arrondissements. I want them cross-referenced with financial records, guest lists, and newsworthy sightings. I want boots at every site within forty-eight hours. Staff placement. Discreet."

The attendant nodded, already lifting a lightweight tablet and activating a secure data link. "Understood. Operatives or freelancers?"

"Both," Dhalia replied. "Freelancers inside. Operatives watching from beyond. And one specialist... at each location. For improvisation, if needed."

"Prioritize high-visibility locations," Dhalia continued. "Anywhere he preens. Anywhere he feeds his image."

Her tone shifted, silk darkened by intent.

"For each establishment, I want one operative embedded—waitstaff, sous chef, valet, maître d', I don't care. Rotate every three days. They don't observe. They serve. Quietly."

The attendant's stylus flicked across the screen in efficient strokes.

"If any of them are touched, kissed, or propositioned—record it. If any of them see him accompanied—catalog the companion. And if any of them are invited to leave with him..." Dhalia paused, turning slightly, the light glancing off her cheekbone like a blade.

"...they may entertain him. If they are willing."

The attendant's eyes flicked up—just once.

"Use the Orpheus Protocol," Dhalia added, more softly now. "Tell them: no marks. No weapons. No deaths. This isn't about fear."

She turned back to the veil and finally, finally, touched it.

"It's about appetite."

There was no warmth in her smile. Only purpose.

"Jules wants a goddess," she said. "Let's show him what devotion costs."

The attendant nodded and vanished as quietly as she had arrived.

Dhalia remained standing alone in the center of the chamber, veil in one hand, mask in the other.

She was the knife.

She was the altar.

And now, she would become the invitation.

She stood before the mirror that showed nothing.

No reflection.

No past.

Just the storm that had survived fire.

Her voice came like dusk—low, velvet-dark, and edged with venom too elegant to scream. She spoke—not to the room, but to the shape of her vengeance.

"He thinks he's collecting a prize.

But what he's getting… is Pandora's Box.

I will starve his empire—not with haste, but with hunger.

Drain his coffers while smiling across a café table.

Bleed his contacts dry—one by one—until even his most loyal begin to vanish.

He'll wake in a fortress turned mausoleum and not know where the rot began.

He'll smell smoke where there's only silence.

Then, I'll take his name.

His reach. His legacy.

I will unravel the silk he wraps around his monster and make the world watch him squirm in the light."

"Jules Devereux traffics in flesh.

In stolen breath. In girlhoods packed into crates. In laughter stripped to silence and invoices.

He took them from my second home—Japan.

Because men like him always circle where the world forgets to look.

But I look.

And I remember.

And so do the ghosts he tried to sell.

He sells what he cannot understand: obedience, elegance, innocence."

Her fingers hovered above the crimson veil.

A breath.

A vow.

"I will burn him from the inside out.

And I will do it in red.

When the last mirror shows him a stranger—when there is nothing left to sell, no name left to barter—

then I'll kill him.

Slowly.

Intimately.

Not with rage. With precision.

Only after he begs for the silence I'll deny him.

Only after he's been made bare.

Because death should be a gift.

And he's earned the long wait to receive it."

Outside the mirrored silence of Dhalia's lair, morning bled slow and grey over the Devereux estate. A fortress of glass, marble, and hidden corridors, it stood aloof behind wrought-iron gates in the 7th arrondissement—designed not just to protect, but to impress.

The courtyard was still.

Until the knock.

Not a hand. A body.

Slumped at the base of the grand stone steps like an offering from the underworld. Sedated. Breathing. No blood. No wounds. No identification. Just Mathis Vorel.

Luciano arrived first. "El infierno [Hell]," he muttered, crouching with a precision honed by years of hunting men. He didn't touch Mathis at first—he watched. Only when satisfied no traps were set did his gloved fingers press to the neck.

Pulse. Weak. Steady.

A moment later, the perimeter sensors triggered a silent ping to the internal command system. Lights shifted. Air thickened. Protocol whispered into motion.

Inside, Jules Devereux was already awake.

The crystal tumbler in his hand met the edge of the fireplace with a crack that sang like broken trust. Bourbon and glass scattered over marble. He stood shirtless in the morning chill, tension wound into every line of his sculpted form. Jules made his way to the atrium where his staff awaited. Silent. Unnerved.

"Where," he growled, "is my fucking security?"

No one dared answer.

Luciano stepped through the doorway like a shadow uncoiling. "He's alive," he said.

Jules's gaze snapped to him. "Who is it?"

Luciano didn't blink. "Mathis Vorel."

A silence fell. Not disbelief. Calculation.

"Bring him inside. Quietly."

Luciano nodded. Two guards moved to retrieve Mathis, lifting his limp body without ceremony.

Jules turned to the nearest control panel and deactivated the alarms manually. His fingers paused over the biometric lock, then clenched.

Luciano watched him in silence.

Jules exhaled. Long. Shallow. Then he turned sharply to the window— glaring not through it, but at it, as if daring the glass to reflect a weakness.

"This wasn't random," he said, pacing once.

"No," Luciano said coolly.

Jules's voice lowered to a knife's edge. "Someone left him there. Not dead. Not hidden. Like a fucking dog at my gates."

"Deliberate," Luciano agreed. "And clean."

Jules's jaw flexed. Fury vibrated just beneath the skin, but he swallowed it like acid. "Put him in the south chamber. I want him upright and lucid when he wakes. No sedation."

Luciano raised a brow. "Interrogator?"

"Now," Jules snapped. Then, quieter—more composed. "Strip him bare. Mentally. Physically. If he remembers anything, I want it recorded."

"And if he doesn't?"

Jules's eyes met his. Glacial. Vicious. "Make him wish he did."

Elsewhere, deeper in the estate—

The fire was quieter here. Smaller. Contained in a private study lined with dark oak and books that looked untouched but weren't. The air smelled of bergamot, smoke, and steel.

Jules stood with his back to the hearth, flamelight flickering across the paneled walls. A decanter of bourbon rested beside a row of antique pistols, but his gaze didn't touch them. Only the glass. Only the reflection.

Gone was the cold grandeur of the atrium. This space was darker, more intimate—leather and mahogany stitched together by the faint hiss of concealed vents. Surveillance feeds pulsed silently along one wall.

Luciano stood still, the hearth casting sharp shadows across his face. He didn't flinch as Jules's gaze snapped to him, sharp and seething.

"You've had eight days," Jules said, voice soft, corroded with threat. "And still no results. No names. No fucking fingerprints. So tell me—what exactly is *El Cazador* hunting?"

Luciano didn't blink. "A phantom. Which means it's real. Just well-fed."

Jules stepped forward, bare feet silent on the marble. "You promised movement. You promised clarity."

"It's in motion," Luciano said. "Two channels are tightening. One in Berlin. The other in Kyoto. She's careful. But her hand will slip."

Jules's nostrils flared. "Then pull it from her wrist and hand it to me."

Luciano's voice was cool iron. "I will."

A beat passed. The only sound was the low hum of the recalibrating security system.

Jules turned sharply, pacing to the liquor cabinet. He poured an inch of bourbon—this time, steady.

"When it does, I don't want whispers. I want screams. I want her dragged from whatever den she thinks makes her clever and shown what precision really looks like."

"She'll break," Luciano said. "They all do."

Jules looked back, the glass glinting in his hand. "No. Not her. She doesn't want a seat at the table—she wants to flip it and slit every throat that ever dined there."

Luciano stepped forward, adjusting his gloves. "Which is why you hired me."

Jules held his stare. Then nodded once.

"Good. Because I'm done entertaining ghosts."

Elsewhere, beneath the weight of Parisian dawn…

Camellia stood alone in her penthouse's upper studio, the one room not touched by Vivianne's precise order. Here, the windows stretched from floor to sky, glass veiled in frost from the early morning chill. A single cup of tea sat untouched on the table beside her. It had long gone cold.

She didn't move.

Not yet.

Below her, the city murmured—car horns, footsteps, the restless stir of a world that never stopped watching. But up here, the silence was curated. Heavy. Intentional.

She wore black—not mourning, not armor, but something in between. Silk clung to her curves like breath withheld. Her hair was coiled high, severe but elegant, the kind of style that dared the world to look twice.

Her eyes weren't on the city.

They were on the mirror.

The same one Maris had once stood before, half-dressed, laughing at nothing. The same one Alex had tried to avoid—because reflections were dangerous things.

Camellia didn't smile.

Her fingers, still ink-smudged from reviewing forged gallery invoices at dawn, traced the edge of the glass. Her reflection stared back—composed, poised, but not at peace. Not anymore.

There were bruises the mirror never showed.

Not on skin—but beneath.

Bruises left by silence. By absence.

By a name she still could not say aloud.

Dhalia.

Her twin was dead.

She was supposed to be dead.

But now—now, the world was beginning to shiver. Not loudly. Not overtly. But in those thin, precise ways only the haunted notice: a shadow that stood too long, a turn of phrase she hadn't heard in years, a scent—faint and floral— that had no place lingering in the gallery halls.

And that woman in red.

The one from the masquerade.

Camellia still couldn't place her. Couldn't explain why her presence had felt like déjà vu torn open at the seams. Vivianne had tried—*was* trying—to uncover her identity, and yet nothing surfaced. No guest list, no footage, no facial match. A ghost in crimson.

And still, Camellia *felt* her.

Not in memory, but in marrow.

Something was off. Rotting. Blooming.

She pressed her palm against the mirror, as if searching for heat behind glass, but her own reflection stared back—elegant, cold, and cracking beneath the surface.

Get ahead of it, she told herself. *Before it consumes you.*

But her hand fell away.

She turned instead toward the partition and crossed into the darker half of her penthouse—where the remnants of the breach were still laid bare: the unlocked drawer, the displaced files, the sealed letter she hadn't dared open again. Until now.

The flash drive waited, untouched on the desk beside it.

She sank into the chair slowly, silk whispering against the leather, and reached for the letter with a hesitation that felt foreign. Her fingers trembled—but only slightly. Enough to know control was no longer absolute.

Camellia unfolded the page.

Read the words.

And read them again.

She couldn't breathe. Not properly.

Across the room, Vivianne stood in stillness. Not interrupting. Not intruding. But watching—with the gaze of someone who had seen art fracture from the inside.

The flash drive's cold weight pressed into Camellia's palm.

Something was unraveling.

And it wasn't just the truth.

It was *her.*

Camellia's pulse tightened beneath her skin.

The masquerade had shaken something loose. Not just in the gallery—but in her.

Her gaze stayed fixed on the flash drive as if it might burn through her skin. It didn't.

It just… waited.

Camellia blinked once—slow, deliberate—and then looked up.

"Vivianne," she said, her voice quieter than usual. No command in it. No veneer. Just her name, spoken like a hand extended across a dark room.

Vivianne stepped forward without hesitation, her heels making no sound against the hardwood. She paused a respectful distance away.

Camellia met her eyes.

"Closer."

It wasn't an order. It was a request.

Vivianne obeyed.

Only then did Camellia speak again, softer now—raw silk unraveling.

"I can't do this alone tonight."

A flicker passed across Vivianne's face. Not surprise. Not pity. Just... understanding. The kind that didn't ask questions.

Camellia held up the flash drive between two fingers. It caught the light like a blade.

"It was left for me. Hidden. With the letter."

Vivianne's eyes lowered to the desk. She saw the envelope. The broken seal. The familiar crest.

"Have you read it?" she asked.

Camellia nodded. "Twice. And I still don't know what it means."

She leaned back in her chair and turned the flash drive over once, then pushed it across the glass surface toward Vivianne. "I want you to see it with me. Every frame. Every file. I trust your mind more than my own right now."

Vivianne's throat moved, but no sound came. She accepted the flash drive with both hands, like something sacred. Then walked wordlessly to the private terminal mounted into the far wall.

Camellia stood and followed, trailing behind like something suspended in water.

The lights dimmed automatically as Vivianne entered her credentials. Camellia hovered close—closer than usual—as if proximity might ward off ghosts.

They watched the screen together.

Not breathing.

Not blinking.

As the first encrypted folder unfolded and a name appeared in flickering text—one neither of them recognized, but both *felt*—Camellia whispered, just loud enough for Vivianne to hear:

"This isn't just about the past."

Vivianne's reply was soft, steady.

"No. It's about what's coming."

And then—

Silence.

Only the glow of the screen.

Only the beginning.

Chapter Fifteen: Mirror Reversal

The Michelin stars didn't twinkle. They burned.

Les Arcanes, nestled in a courtyard just off Rue de l'Université, was more temple than restaurant. Shadow-drenched alcoves, hand-blown crystal chandeliers, and waitstaff that moved like water over glass. The clientele glittered: ambassadors, heiresses, cartel liaisons dressed like art dealers. And tonight, among them, sat the devil himself.

Jules Devereux occupied his usual corner table—one where his back could never be exposed. The lighting obeyed him. The waitstaff knew not to linger. He drank a Saint-Émilion that cost more than most lives, swirling it with the indolent confidence of a man who thought he owned time.

Until she arrived.

She did not *enter* so much as she *arrived*.

Crimson.

The dress was simplicity draped in sin. Silk that clung without desperation, hinting at the curves it did not expose, save for the delicate rise of cleavage and the precise taper of her waist. Black Louboutin heels caught the light with every step. Her hair was pinned in soft waves, just unruly enough to suggest defiance.

The hostess blinked, caught mid-word.

"Mademoiselle…"

"Valencia," Dhalia said with a gentle, honeyed smile. "Seraphine Valencia." The lie tasted exquisite.

She was led to a table deliberately chosen hours before. Not too close. Not too far. Diagonal to Jules' line of sight. When she sat, her silhouette became geometry: all clean lines, dangerous curves, and crimson promise.

She didn't look at him.

But she knew the moment he noticed.

The weight of his stare pressed against her bare shoulder like a dare. She lifted her wineglass—rosé, dry, deliberate—and sipped without acknowledgment.

Five minutes passed.

Then the waiter approached. A vintage Romanée-Conti 1999, uncorked with reverence.

"Compliments of Monsieur Devereux," he murmured.

Dhalia turned her head. Slowly.

Across the room, Jules raised his own glass in a silent toast. He was all silver cufflinks and veiled hunger. Controlled. Polished. Predictable.

She allowed the corners of her mouth to lift—not a smile. A concession.

She did not toast back.

The meal unfolded in small bites: saffron scallops, fig-glazed duck, whisper-thin sheets of truffle pasta. Dhalia ate like a woman unbothered by time or attention. Her gaze skimmed the restaurant, always returning to her wine, her fork, the unread book beside her plate.

Finally, he came.

"Mademoiselle Valencia."

His voice was low, cultured silk soaked in cognac.

She looked up with studied ease. "Monsieur…?"

"Devereux. Jules."

She tilted her head, a crescent of interest arcing through her features. "Ah. My benefactor."

He bowed slightly. "It seemed criminal for a woman in crimson to dine unaccompanied."

"Some criminals leave deeper marks."

Jules chuckled. "Do you always dine alone, Miss Valencia?"

"Only when I wish to be seen."

He offered his hand. She didn't take it.

"Are you here for the cuisine, or the company?"

"Tonight? The ambiance. Tomorrow?" She smiled, slow as poison. "Who knows."

He lowered his voice. "Would you consider dessert elsewhere?"

"Tempting. But dangerous."

"Danger can be sweet."

She stood, gathering her clutch.

"So can restraint."

He watched her leave. No card. No number. Just a name that didn't exist and a scent that lingered like prophecy.

Later.

The moon peeled silver across the windows of a black car parked in the alley behind *Les Arcanes*. Dhalia sat inside, legs crossed, veil once again untouched beside her. The heels were off. Her bare feet flexed slightly against the cool leather floor.

She tapped the encrypted comm line herself. It flared to life.

"Kenji. Report."

His voice came steady. "Assets mobilizing. Our contact in the 8th arrondissement confirmed visual on Devereux's regular staff rotations. We're mapping patterns."

"Good."

"Your end?"

Dhalia's lips curled, slow and venomous. "The bait took himself. He approached within the hour. Tracked me. Toasted me. Invited me."

"Did you accept?"

"I denied him... seductively. He's agitated. Interested. Predictably arrogant."

"Phase two?"

"Begin cross-channel embedding," she ordered. "I want at least two of our people on his estate staff within seventy-two hours. Nannies, assistants, caterers—whatever gets them inside. Use Orpheus protocol for identity creation. Rotate identities every twelve days. No pattern exposure."

"Yes, ma'am."

She glanced out the window, to the glowing rooftop across the street. Her reflection barely touched the glass.

"And Kenji... bring Alex."

"Coordinates?"

Her voice was final. "The theatre. Same stage."

"Understood."

The line went dead without ceremony.

Dhalia reclined, slipping back into her heels as if preparing for war.

Tonight was a taste.

Tomorrow, she would dine.

But beneath the silk and candlelight, something else had awakened—

Not hunger. Not vengeance. A reckoning.

And reckoning doesn't knock.

It enters like a mirror breaking from the inside.

The heels clicked once more against the cobblestone street—no longer for seduction, but declaration.

She was no longer watching the game.

She was walking into it.

By morning, her name would vanish from reservation books and camera feeds.

By dusk, it would be on the lips of men who didn't yet know they were bleeding.

Seraphine Valencia was the mask.

But Dhalia Solé was the blade.

And blades do not knock.

They slip between ribs.

Smiling.

The night air had changed.

It carried something heavier than perfume. Something unsaid but not unscented—like the memory of blood rinsed from marble. Paris hadn't noticed yet. But it would. The city would feel her eventually.

Dhalia didn't walk through shadows. She carried them.

The echo of her heels in the corridor beneath *Les Arcanes* still lingered, soft as a threat. She hadn't left a calling card. Just a ripple in the atmosphere—felt by every eye that followed her out and every man who wondered what had just passed him by.

Above her, Devereux drank from the glass she didn't toast. He was already marked. Not by lipstick. Not by fingerprints. But by attention—hers. She'd chosen her stage and made her entrance.

Now, the velvet tightened.

Elsewhere, Camellia stood at the edge of her own knowing. Unaware, but not untouched.

The flash drive was back on her desk—its matte black shell nestled like a thorn in the center of her meticulously ordered workspace. The seal was broken. The letter still unopened, though it pressed against the edges of her peripheral vision like a dare.

Vivianne had already fired up the security console—reinitiating the encrypted system that Camellia insisted remain air-gapped except in moments like these. Moments that felt less like decisions and more like unraveling necessity.

Camellia inserted the drive without ceremony.

The screen blinked once. Then again.

Lines of code spilled across the monitor like ink in water—too fast, too dense, too intentional.

Vivianne leaned in. "It's indexing."

Camellia said nothing, her eyes locked on the screen as the console's cooling system kicked into a low hum. The silence was no longer comfortable—it pulsed.

Then the screen split.

Folders bloomed like spores: no names, just static. No clear path. The system seemed to hang for a moment—then quietly began its work.

But it wasn't just opening. It was embedding.

Unnoticed.

Deep in the background, the drive's true payload deployed—quiet code threading through gallery firewalls like smoke under a locked door. It tapped into archived footage, decrypted dormant files, pulled stills from years Camellia had tried to forget.

No alerts. No red flags. The system didn't resist—it welcomed.

Then, without prompting, a series of images bloomed across the screen.

Camellia, in the mirrored room. Her body wrapped in shadow and reflection. Maris's fingers along her spine. Alex's mouth at her throat. A kiss half-finished, a sigh turned confession.

The images were not security footage. They were curated. Selected. Precise.

Then—

Japan. Over a year ago. A blurred shot of Camellia and Maris beneath red paper lanterns. Fingers intertwined. A moment no camera should've caught.

Next—

Her bedroom. Just after the masquerade. Alex on his knees. Camellia with her head thrown back, eyes shut, vulnerable.

She stepped back. Her breath stuttered.

Vivianne stood frozen, not daring to move.

"It's pulling from hidden systems," Vivianne said. "These angles... they aren't from us."

Camellia's voice broke. "Then from where?"

No answer came. Only more snapshots. More intimacy rendered into surveillance.

The gallery's lighting flickered. Only slightly. Unnoticeable to most. But not to them.

Vivianne reached for the command console. "I'll isolate—"

"No," Camellia said. Her voice trembled, but she was firm. "Let it finish."

The images continued—each one more intimate, more invasive. Dhalia's signature was nowhere. But her presence was everywhere.

The drive had already woven itself into the gallery's nervous system. There was no extraction. Only infection.

Camellia's hands curled against the desk. Vivianne stepped beside her. They said nothing.

The curator had become the exhibit. And the theatre had a new director.

The gallery, once sacred, now pulsed like a wound.

Its heartbeat wasn't hers anymore. Not entirely.

Somewhere else in the city, another pulse quickened.

161

The order had been clear.

Bring Alex.

Kenji didn't ask questions. Dhalia's voice, when it dropped, to that low-honeyed register—just above a whisper, just below a threat—left no room for interpretation. *The theatre. Same stage.* That was all she said. And it was enough.

He drove a black coupe that didn't hum—it glided. Matte, untagged, anonymous. Tonight wasn't for being seen. It was for being remembered.

He found Alex in the Marais, stepping out of a café as if nothing in his world was unraveling. Fresh shirt, clean lines, cologne still clinging to a hope he didn't realize was already ash in someone else's hand. He looked like a man trying to reclaim control. Or perform it.

He didn't notice the car until it stopped directly in front of him.

The window rolled down, just enough.

"Get in," Kenji said.

Alex blinked. "What?"

"Now."

There was no title, no threat. Just that voice—flat, unyielding, familiar.

Alex didn't move. "You're not even going to tell me why?"

Kenji leaned an elbow on the steering wheel. "You've been summoned."

"By who?"

Kenji didn't answer. He didn't need to. He only held Alex's gaze with the weight of inevitability. That was worse than a name.

Alex glanced up and down the street. It was reflex. No one was watching. But that didn't mean no one was listening.

Finally, he opened the door and slipped inside.

The car closed around him like a verdict.

Kenji said nothing. Neither did the engine. It whispered across the cobblestone, slipping through Paris with ghostlike precision. Streetlights blurred into streaks of amber and frost. They slipped past the shuttered cafes of Rue des Rosiers and under Metro Line 1, the city humming just above. The theatre was buried behind a closed spice shop—its façade faded to anonymity, its secrets curated beneath. Alex's fingers tapped once against his knee, then stopped.

"Is this about Camellia?" he finally asked, quieter now.

Still no answer.

Kenji's eyes never left the road.

They crossed into a forgotten arrondissement, where the buildings leaned like secrets and the air tasted like abandoned time. At the end of an alley, wrapped in the lie of renovation, the theatre waited—darkened façade, scaffolding like a spider's grip.

Kenji killed the engine. Stepped out. Opened Alex's door.

Alex didn't move right away.

"I don't even know who I'm meeting," he said.

Kenji tilted his head. "You will."

A pause.

"Should I be afraid?"

Kenji looked at him fully then, his expression unreadable.

"That depends," he said, "on how honest you've been."

Alex swallowed hard. Then stepped out of the car.

The theatre loomed ahead—quiet, watching, wide-mouthed in its silence.

And the city, just behind them, pretended not to notice.

The theatre looked abandoned from the outside—a carcass dressed in scaffolding, its marquee letters long since vanished. But as Kenji led him past the rusted gate and beneath the illusion of disrepair, something shifted. The darkness wasn't empty. It was waiting.

Alex's steps echoed too loudly against the tiled foyer. His hands flexed once at his sides, instinct twitching against restraint. The air was cooler here. Heavy with the scent of velvet dust and ghosted perfumes.

Kenji moved ahead without glancing back. The silence was ceremonial.

They descended a short corridor—bare bulbs flickering in intervals overhead—until a set of double doors opened into a world Alex didn't expect.

The theatre was alive.

Ornate. Candlelit. Draped in crimson and shadows.

A single stage light glowed at the center, casting a soft circle against a

163

backdrop of red velvet curtains. The seats were empty, but the presence was undeniable. Something breathed here. Something watched.

"Go," Kenji said.

Alex turned to him, uncertainty crawling up his spine.

"She's waiting."

Alex crossed the threshold alone.

Each step toward the stage felt like a surrender. He swallowed hard, scanning the theatre's edges for movement, but found none. The spotlight warmed his skin, but the rest of the room remained cool, hungry.

And then she appeared.

Not from the shadows. From above.

Dhalia descended from the opera box—her silhouette gliding along the stairwell like a verse sung in slow-motion. She wore silk the color of midnight wine. Her hair fell in decadent waves, the kind that took hours to pin, then more to free. No jewelry. No need.

She didn't smile.

"Alex," she said. Like she already knew how he tasted.

He turned sharply.

"You…"

"Me," she confirmed. Her voice was low and lilting, each word deliberate. She circled him slowly, eyes raking over every inch. "You've been very busy."

He stiffened. "You're the one behind all of it. The files. The surveillance. The drugs."

"Behind?" She laughed, soft and cruel. "Darling, I *am* it."

She stopped in front of him.

"And you? You've been such a lovely little thread in my tapestry. So eager to please. So easy to position."

"I didn't know who I was working for."

"No. You only knew what turned you on."

Alex flinched. Her proximity pressed against the edge of his self-control.

Dhalia lifted a hand, brushed a lock of hair from his forehead. He didn't pull away. Not because he didn't want to. Because he couldn't.

"Camellia made you feel seen," she murmured. "But only because she needed a mirror."

He tried to speak. She touched his lips.

"Shh. Let me show you what it means to be devoured."

Her touch lingered. Not possessive—inevitable.

He swallowed hard. "Why me?"

Dhalia's eyes glittered like wet garnet in low light. "Because you wobble so beautifully on the edge of control."

She walked a slow circle around him again. "Camellia gave you form. I will give you *freedom.*"

His breath caught.

She tilted her head. "You betrayed her with your gaze. With your doubts. With your *mouth.*"

Alex faltered.

Dhalia leaned closer. "You already chose, Alex. I'm simply giving your choice a stage."

And in that moment, he understood. The scattered whispers. The half-truths. The orders relayed through faceless channels. The drugs, the dossiers, the missions that reeked of two opposing scents.

It was now clear.

The woman behind the mask, the true conductor of the chaos—was Dhalia.

His chest rose in a slow, shallow breath.

"I work for you," he said quietly. Not a question.

Dhalia smiled. "You always have."

The spotlight above warmed him, softened his edges. The rest of the theatre was cool, waiting.

She studied him—not with hunger, but precision. This wasn't seduction. This was alignment. A marionette discovering its strings.

"You want to be good," she whispered. "But oh, how the *bad* suits you."

He didn't respond.

She didn't need him to.

"Camellia offered you… order. I offer you chaos. Which one makes you feel *alive?*"

He clenched his jaw.

She smiled.

"Exactly."

She circled back to face him. "You are going to help me, Alex. Not because I asked. But because something inside you *aches* to be told what to do."

Her fingers ghosted down his chest. "I will give you purpose. Power. *Pleasure.*"

She leaned in.

"And in return, you will help me destroy your queen."

His breath came uneven now. He wasn't sure where it began. Or who he was beneath it.

"Why does it have to be me?" he asked, softer this time. Not a question. A tether resisting slack, fraying slowly beneath the gravity of her gaze.

Her lips curved. "You've already begun."

The spotlight dimmed.

The curtain did not fall.

It *burned.*

And beneath the smoldering velvet, a new act waited—one not yet written, but already rehearsed.

Chapter Sixteen: A Flower for the Dead

Smoke curled in delicate threads above the footlights. Somewhere in the distance, a city exhaled beneath moonlit tension. But inside the theatre, the world had narrowed to the sound of Dhalia's heels retreating across the stage and the echo that refused to fade.

Alex remained still, breath shallow, a marionette poised on the verge of collapse.

"Follow me," she said without turning.

He obeyed.

They descended a spiral stairwell behind the stage, deeper into the theatre's bones. Velvet gave way to concrete. Opulence faded into dust. And then— a room.

Spartan. Industrial. A low table, two chairs, and a carafe of dark wine that had not been poured.

Dhalia gestured to a seat. Not an offer. A command.

He sat.

She poured only for herself.

"Do you know what it's like," she began, her voice almost too soft, "to grow up beside someone with the same eyes, the same blood, but not the same origin?"

Alex didn't speak. But something flickered behind his eyes. Not confusion— recognition. Not empathy—unease.

"My mother was not Camellia's mother," Dhalia continued. "That truth was hidden in whispers, and sealed in files no one thought I'd learn to read. But I did. Because I had to."

She sipped the wine.

"Camellia was sunlight. Curated. Protected. I was the shadow that proved her glow. I was always told to sit quieter. Dress simpler. Smile less. Because one rose was enough for the garden."

Her nails tapped the glass—sharp, staccato.

"My grandmother hated me. I didn't understand it at first. I thought I just wasn't lovable. I tried so hard to earn something—approval, affection, anything. But all I earned were bruises that faded and words that didn't."

A silence settled. She didn't blink.

"She'd call me her reminder. Her mistake. Said my existence was a stain on the Solé legacy. That no man's lapse in judgment should walk around bearing her family name. I was starved of softness. Punished for presence. I was locked in rooms for speaking out of turn. I was made to kneel in gravel when I forgot to call her 'Madame.'"

Alex's jaw clenched.

"But my father..." Dhalia's voice softened. A breath, almost tender. "He tried. He held me when I cried and told me stories of flowers that only bloomed in fire. He'd smuggle sweets under the library staircase, teach me how to draw birds in the margins of ledgers. He gave me my first real smile. And for a time, I believed that love could be enough."

She paused, fingers curling slightly around the stem of her glass.

"Camellia and I... we were inseparable once. She used to braid my hair in the sunroom. We'd whisper poems to each other after dark. We built forts out of bedsheets and swore we'd never be apart."

She looked down, a flash of something wounded breaking across her features.

"But my grandmother knew how to separate blooms. She called it pruning. She started isolating us—feeding Camellia ideas about refinement, legacy, poise. Told her that I would ruin her future. That I wasn't truly her sister. Just the body that shared her birthday."

Alex looked away, chest tight.

"Camellia pulled back. Not because she stopped loving me. But because she started fearing what loving me would cost. I watched her become what they wanted. And I—"

She exhaled, bitter.

"I became what they feared."

The flame on the candle danced, restless.

"They tried to erase me. Hide me. Burn me."

Her voice didn't crack, but her hand trembled.

"And maybe they would have… if Kenji's family hadn't found me."

She set the wine down, untouched since that first sip.

"His uncle was paid to kill me," Dhalia said, the words emerging not with anger, but with the steadiness of a scar that no longer bled. "Not scare. Not warn. Kill."

She looked down at her wine glass but didn't drink. The candlelight etched the hollow of her throat in shadow.

"The fire was meant to be thorough. My grandmother was never careless when it came to disposal. My room—drenched in accelerant, corners soaked like parchment dipped in kerosene. The mattress, the books, even the dolls she allowed me—every thread of softness, flammable. Erasable."

Her voice didn't shake. But the air around her changed. Denser. Charged.

"She called it pruning the tree. I was the rot she swore would ruin the Solé name if allowed to bloom. The bastard daughter of a man who wandered. A living error. An inconvenience that cried and bled and smiled like it belonged."

Her gaze flicked to the candle again. The flame swayed, its light a weak echo of the inferno she described.

"They waited until nightfall. Until the staff rotated. Until Camellia had been tucked into bed two rooms over with a kiss and a bedtime story about swans. And then… he came."

She drew a slow breath.

"His uncle. Kenji's blood. A man with a quiet soul and a brutal job. He had a photograph. A lighter. A silencer, in case the smoke didn't do its job quickly enough. And yet—"

Her jaw set.

"He opened the door and saw a child. Curled on a floor with singed braids and a half-read fairy tale in her lap. Not a traitor. Not a threat. Just a little girl they'd rather see dead than acknowledged."

Alex's throat was dry. He didn't dare move.

"And maybe it was pity," she said. "Or the sound I made when I saw him—a gasp that wasn't fear, but hope. Or maybe he looked at me and didn't see a body to burn. Maybe he saw a blade waiting to be honed."

Her eyes were black with memory.

"He didn't light the match. He wrapped me in his coat. Carried me out through the servants' passage as the room behind us ignited. And from that moment, I was no longer a Solé."

She sat the glass down.

"I became Moriyama. Not by name. By purpose. They didn't cradle me. They forged me. Every bruise became a lesson. Every silence, a signal. I learned to speak without sound. To vanish in mirrors. To return as someone else."

Her eyes locked on Alex.

"Camellia mourned a ghost. Held funerals in her dreams. But I—"

She leaned forward, voice lowering to a whisper jagged with fire.

"I was learning how to haunt."

Alex didn't flinch—but something in him uncoiled. The rawness of her words had opened a wound he hadn't known still bled. His throat tightened. His palms prickled.

He saw it now. Not just the scar. But the scalpel.

Not just the fire.

But the girl they tried to burn.

And he—

He felt himself sway.

Toward her.

Toward the wreckage. Toward the myth.

Alex leaned back slightly, the chair creaking under his weight. The flickering candlelight traced the sharp lines of his jaw, but his expression had softened.

He wasn't afraid of her.

He was afraid of how much of himself he saw in her.

He thought of his own blurred loyalties. Of all the orders followed without names. Of all the mirrors he had looked into and failed to recognize the man behind them. He had spent so long looking for purpose in Camellia's world—curated, composed, and tightly wound.

But here—

Here, in this room of exposed concrete and confession—

Here, Dhalia bled truth like a blade drawn slow.

And Alex felt it.

Felt the pull.

"Do you understand now, Alex? This isn't revenge. This is resurrection."

He met her eyes.

And in them, he saw not grief—but rebirth.

Not ashes.

But fire.

He exhaled—slowly, deeply. Something in him released. Not allegiance. Not surrender. But curiosity. Dangerous, delicious curiosity.

"You survived them," he said quietly.

Her lips barely moved. "No. I outlived them."

Another pause.

"You said Camellia offered me form. And you... freedom. But what if I want something else entirely?"

Dhalia tilted her head, amused. "Then you're already mine."

The candle guttered. The air shifted.

And somewhere beneath the city, the echo of two ghosts began to merge.

Not as twins.

As rivals.

As reflections.

As resurrection.

The silence between them pulsed—thick, suggestive, an atmosphere charged like storm-lit velvet.

Dhalia rose slowly, taking her wine glass with her. Her silhouette cleaved through the shadows with a regal menace. She didn't walk—she prowled, every step soaked in deliberation and promise, until she loomed before him like a verdict.

Alex didn't breathe.

She let her fingers trail over his shoulder—languid, possessive, the way fire teases skin just before it sears. Then, like silk succumbing to gravity, she straddled his lap.

The chair groaned. So did something in him.

Her thighs bracketed him with slow, knowing pressure. Her body hovered—denial crafted into proximity, a tease so precise it demanded obedience. One hand cradled her glass like a ritual blade. The other traced the slope of his chest, slipping beneath his collar with a heat that was almost cruel.

"For every inch you take from her," she purred, each syllable a caress, "you'll earn a piece of me."

Her words melted against his skin like dark chocolate in flame.

The rim of her glass kissed his lips—then his jaw—then dipped toward his throat.

"You'll listen," she continued, low and opulent. "You'll observe. You'll seduce her silence until it screams."

A drop of wine escaped her mouth. It glided down the curve of her neck, lingered at the valley between her breasts, and disappeared into the silk below.

"You'll become the itch she can't soothe. The ache she names in her sleep."

She leaned in—so close, the heat of her breath turned the air electric.

"And when she begs—on her knees, voice raw with need—I'll show you what it means to be truly claimed."

Her hips shifted. His pulse followed.

Her hand wandered lower, each inch a challenge, until her palm rested against the heat that had risen between them.

"You'll feel me," she whispered into his neck, "in every lie you tell her... and every truth you swallow for me."

She didn't kiss him.

She burned him—without flame, without mercy, just presence.

Her gaze caught his, sharp with hunger, thick with dominance.

"I don't want your loyalty, Alex."

Her fingers curled.

"I want your undoing."

And in his breathless stillness, she tasted it.

Then she rose, fluid as smoke, leaving heat and silence in her wake.

Alex exhaled as if released from a spell.

From the shadows beyond the corridor, the sound of approaching footsteps echoed with surgical precision.

Kenji.

He appeared without ceremony, but his presence was definitive. Always the scalpel. Never the stitch.

Dhalia didn't turn to him.

"Take him back," she said simply.

Kenji nodded, gaze brushing Alex like a blade checking for cracks.

Alex stood slowly. His limbs felt heavier than before—warmer, looser, like they remembered her weight and resented the absence.

He didn't speak.

Neither did she.

Dhalia disappeared into the corridor behind the flickering candlelight, her wine glass still half full, her stride untouched. The concrete gave way to velvet again. Then glass. Then light.

Her driver waited.

So did the private suite high above the Place Vendôme, where gowns hung like weapons and perfumes lined the counter like poisons. Her hair was unbound. Her body, unreadied. But her mind—already dressed for war.

She would see Jules again.

Not as bait.

Not yet as closure.

But the noose was already woven—

Silk-wrapped. Perfumed. And patient.

And when he finally looked into her eyes...

He wouldn't see a woman.

He'd see the reckoning he never prepared for.

Chapter Seventeen: The Quiet Knife

The Parisian dusk was deceptive—brushed in gold, whispering calm. But beneath that warmth, the city murmured in voltage and venom. Circuits carried secrets like veins carry blood, and tonight, someone's heart was about to stop.

Miles below the surface, beneath layers of architecture and anonymity, in a bunker disguised as maintenance infrastructure, a name pulsed softly on a glass screen—subtle, but damning.

Vivianne Marchand.

Luciano Navarro didn't blink. He didn't need to. The name filtered into his mind the way blood scent does to a predator—unmistakable. His gloved hand hovered over a digital thread projected from a needle-thin console strapped to his wrist, the interface blooming into existence with a muted hiss.

"Éste huele a seda y mentiras," he murmured. *This one smells like silk and lies.*

The room around him wasn't just dark—it was engineered black, a shade so deep it consumed reflection and memory alike. The kind of place built to erase presence.

Beside him stood two operatives—his finest ghosts. Unnamed. Untraceable. The woman to his left had once collapsed a surveillance ring in Seoul without leaving her seat. The man to his right had no known voiceprint. Together, they didn't breathe unless Luciano allowed it.

"Timeline?" he asked without turning.

The woman responded, her voice sharp enough to cut glass. "Initial breach: ten days ago. Two hundred forty hours. The hacker rerouted through mirrored nodes, used corrupted MACs, and masked the origin with a single-direction relay bouncing through Barcelona."

A beat.

"Source path terminates at Galerie Solé."

Luciano's mouth twitched. Not a smile—more like the memory of one. "Show me."

With a flick of her fingers, a holographic overlay unfolded in the air—schematics of the gallery, surveillance archives, heat-mapped anomalies. The digital architecture shimmered like a temple made of code and sin.

One anomaly emerged. A figure. Constant. Efficient. Predictable. But never quite there.

Vivianne Marchand.

She never used the main entrances. Her routes were clockwork—too disciplined. Her patterns lacked the chaos of guilt, but also the spontaneity of innocence. Luciano's eyes narrowed on the timestamps when she was absent. They aligned with breach spikes.

Those were the nights he liked best.

"She's clean," the other agent said. "Too clean. Rotates passwords every seventy-two hours. Separate biometrics per device. Routine suggests OCD-level structure. She's not the hacker."

A pause.

"She's the conduit."

Luciano's eyes turned colder than glass in a morgue. "And conduits bleed just the same."

He closed the projection with a flick. The data collapsed silently, like a verdict carried out in darkness.

"Locate. Follow." A pause. Then, flatly: "Do not touch."

Elsewhere in Paris, in the underbelly of a boutique hotel too old for the internet but too private for questions, Kenji Moriyama stared into a feed tunneled through a one-time pad chain, piggybacked on a QKD test line running off academic fiber. The feed looping across five screens. His own reflection was never among them.

He had been watching since the breach began. Since Jules Devereux muttered through clenched teeth: *Find the snake in my garden.*

Kenji felt it the moment Luciano Navarro joined the hunt. Not through confirmation, but through consequence. Underground forums went silent. False credentials started failing. Known safehouses ghosted themselves off maps. Navarro didn't search.

He *hunted.*

And when he moved, people weren't found again.

Kenji's fingers danced across a darkened keyboard, tracking the rise in surveillance pressure around Galerie Solé. The net was tightening. Vivianne's alias had been pinged once—just once—in a flagged comms packet near Oberkampf. Enough for Luciano's dogs to sniff her out.

Dhalia's voice sliced through the encrypted channel—clear, poised, and deadly.

"Report."

Kenji didn't flinch. "They've found the thread. It leads to Vivianne."

A pause. Just long enough to chill the room.

"She's mine to break," Dhalia said, voice like crushed velvet dipped in arsenic.

Kenji gave the smallest of nods, though she wasn't watching. "Protection order in place. She's already being extracted."

Vivianne moved quickly, heels muffled by sound-dampening soles designed for discretion, not fashion. She didn't run. Running made you prey. But she didn't stroll, either. Her pace was calibrated—neither urgent nor slow. Measured. Intentional. The kind of movement that slipped through alleyways and scrutiny like water through stone.

She was two blocks from her fallback route when the streetlights flickered—not a power surge, but a signal. The kind her training had taught her to recognize before her brain even caught up.

From the side street ahead, a black vehicle glided into view—silent, deliberate. No screech of tires. No wasted motion. The rear door unlocked with a soft mechanical click, timed like breath before a shot.

Vivianne halted. Assessed.

Then came the voice from the shadows inside.

"Get in," said the woman. Low. Clear. Commanding. No name. No time.

Vivianne's gaze swept the street—windows, rooftops, reflections. "Who sent—?"

"I don't have time to explain," the voice snapped, quieter now but edged like broken glass. "If you stay out here ten more seconds, you'll be collateral on Luciano's next report."

That name froze the air for a beat.

Vivianne didn't blink. She calculated—angle of escape, bag weight, exposed skin, wind direction.

Then she got in.

The door shut behind her like a sealed order.

No sooner had the engine ignited than another black vehicle—same make, same color, same plates—roared to life down the block. Inside it, another woman sat in the backseat, shoulders tense, face partially obscured by a cascade of dark curls and tinted sunglasses.

The decoy.

A body double dressed in Vivianne's signature gallery attire—cream blouse, navy slacks, a shawl with gold threading pulled over one shoulder. She even wore Vivianne's scent—one Maris had replicated from dry-cleaning tags and hairbrush fibers collected during a prior recon. Enough to fool cameras. Enough to fool heat scans.

The moment the decoy vehicle peeled off, it cut a corner too fast—on purpose. Enough to draw eyes.

And it worked.

Two unmarked surveillance bikes detached from opposite ends of the block. One overhead drone pivoted, locking on to the speeding twin. Within moments, the chase was on.

Maris didn't look back. She didn't need to.

"That should buy us nine minutes," she murmured.

Vivianne, eyes still forward, spoke evenly. "I'm impressed."

"No," Maris replied, flicking a switch near the gear console. "You're in trouble."

A soft whir passed through the chassis. Beneath them, the flipper rig fed from a pool of real stolen tags, randomly looped. RFID ghosters made it look clean to street-level scanners.

Vivianne allowed herself a glance. "Rotating plates?"

"Minimalist counter-surveillance."

"Government tech," Vivianne said. Not a question.

"No," Maris said again. "It's art."

They turned down a service lane, passed an unmarked maintenance gate, and slipped into the mouth of a forgotten municipal tunnel. A final click locked the car into shadow. The light above them folded into dark.

Inside, silence stretched taut. Not unfamiliar. Not friendly. Just two women bound by the same gravitational force, studying each other through the edges of a mutual myth.

They didn't trust each other.

But now, they were in the same car.

And there was no getting out without revealing the truth.

They entered the safehouse in silence.

No signs. No numbers. Just an unmarked service elevator inside an abandoned transit hub that hadn't seen a real inspector in over a decade. The walls whispered of forgotten floods and ghosted lives. Inside, the air was cold, dry, filtered through underground vents.

The elevator doors opened into a narrow corridor lit with motion-triggered strips. Concrete. Steel. No excess. Just edges and essentials.

Maris keyed in a code, then a retinal scan. The door unlocked with a clean, hydraulic hiss.

The room beyond was sterile but not lifeless. A single desk. A locked storage wall. Two chairs. A secured terminal tucked beneath a transparent polycarbonate hood glowing faint blue. Nothing said "home." Everything said "alive."

Vivianne stepped inside and didn't bother asking questions.

Maris gestured toward the terminal. "You get one call."

Vivianne raised a brow. "Camellia."

"One line. One time. Two minutes," Maris said, voice crisp, already moving to set the encryption barriers and kill any outbound trace. "This system is off-grid and vaporizes its own memory after execution. Once the line drops, it's gone. No re-dials. No do-overs."

Vivianne's fingers flexed at her side.

Maris looked at her. Really looked. "Make it count."

Then she stepped back, arms crossed, eyes cool.

Vivianne sat.

The screen warmed. The countdown began.

02:00

01:59

01:58...

And somewhere across the city, the line to Camellia Solé pulsed alive—sharp as a blade.

Back beneath the Metro—now a kill zone in wait—Luciano moved like smoke under pressure. His boots scuffed soot from decades-old tile. The walls bore scorches of another century. He was alone now. His team fanned out.

"She's moved," said the female agent.

"Where?"

"Unknown. Disappeared off-grid forty-seven minutes ago. Last seen near Rue Oberkampf."

Luciano inhaled. Slow. Deep.

"She's not the snake."

"No?"

"She's the lock."

He pulled a knife from his coat—long, thin, curved at the tip like a question mark.

"And somewhere, there's a key who thinks they're safe. FIND HER!"

A masked figure stepped into view from the shadows. No noise. No tell. Just presence, like gravity forming mid-breath.

Luciano's hand twitched toward his blade.

The masked figure spoke first.

"Turn back, Navarro."

The voice was modulated—clear, even—but artificial. Still, something in the cadence gave Luciano pause.

"Who the fuck are you?"

"You'll figure it out. Eventually. Maybe after I've made sure you don't get close again."

Luciano tilted his head.

"You block my hunt. You wear a mask. You know my name."

He stepped forward. Knife out now, loose in his hand like a promise.

"I don't like riddles."

"And I don't like monsters sniffing at Camellia's door," the masked man replied. Cool. Impossibly still.

Luciano's eyes narrowed. "So this is personal."

"Not yet. But keep walking forward, and it will be."

Luciano smiled—ugly and perfect.

"Most men who threaten me don't live to make a second impression."

Kenji's voice came calm, buried in code.

"Good thing I'm not most men."

Luciano lunged. The clash was instant—blade against twin sai, sparks flickering off metal as the fight drove them down the length of the forgotten platform.

Luciano fought like a surgeon with a vendetta. Kenji blocked like he'd trained in shadows. The knife slashed air; the sai countered, pinned, twisted.

Footsteps echoed. Grunts. Collisions.

The fight shifted again.

Then—Luciano's earpiece crackled to life.

"Target acquired. Visual confirmation. Pursuing."

He froze. Just enough.

Kenji's sai kissed the edge of Luciano's collarbone.

Luciano smirked.

"Another day then," he said, voice low. "Would've liked to see what color you bleed."

He stepped back. Knife still ready, but breath controlled.

Kenji's reply was silence.

Luciano vanished into the fog.

But not without a final look back.

He wanted that fight again.

Far above, in the suite Dhalia kept like a chapel, her reflection watched her from the mirror—not with vanity, but with calculation. One hand traced the stem of a crystal glass. The other hovered above a tablet, glowing dimly with the last known locations of every piece she had placed on the board—her operatives, her assets, her shadows.

Luciano would come again. That much was inevitable.

But she would not meet him.

She would move three steps ahead. Veiled in velvet. Laced in violence. With a name on her tongue and ruin in her wake.

The screen dimmed.

Her lips parted—not for a smile.

For a whisper.

"Let him chase ghosts."

She turned toward the sealed chamber behind her, where a black case waited, biometric lock still glowing red.

Inside it: silk gloves. And the kind of blade not meant to kill quickly.

Chapter Eighteen: House of Solé

The silence in the safehouse wasn't just quiet. It was complete—dense and absolute, like a room padded not for sound but for memory.

Vivianne Marchand sat on the edge of a sterile cot, ceramic cup cupped between elegant hands, long gone cold. The fluorescents buzzed overhead like distant flies. The air smelled faintly of gun oil, antiseptic, and sun-warmed paper—like history left too long in the open. There were no clocks. No windows. Just the pulse of surveillance gear and the hum of a building designed to outlast questions.

Across the room, Maris leaned against the concrete wall with a dancer's stillness, her silhouette all quiet threat and unreadable poise. One boot rested against the wall. Her arms crossed. Her eyes didn't wander.

Neither woman had spoken in five minutes.

It wasn't tension. It was inevitability.

"You're too quiet to be scared," Maris said at last. Her voice, low and lyrical, curled like cigarette smoke. "And too still to be calm. So what are you?"

Vivianne raised her eyes. "Calculating."

That earned the hint of a smile. Maris pushed off the wall and circled slowly. "That makes two of us."

Vivianne took another sip—cool, bitter. "Do you always guard prisoners with riddles and cold tea?"

"Only the ones who might be worth the trouble."

A pause.

"Why me?" Vivianne asked.

Maris didn't sit immediately. She finished her loop, then slid into the chair

182

opposite Vivianne with a languid grace.

"Because she said so."

"Camellia?"

Maris shook her head. "No. The other one."

Vivianne's fingers tightened slightly on the cup.

"Dhalia," she echoed. But this time, it wasn't confirmation. It was suspicion wrapped in disbelief. A name she'd only heard in memories long past. A ghost, not a woman.

Maris gave a solemn nod.

Vivianne's voice lowered. "Camellia never says her name. Only fragments. Ash. Smoke. A wound you don't touch."

"Because she knows it'll bleed," Maris said. "But Dhalia's real. Real enough to command shadows. Real enough to give orders that kill."

Vivianne's gaze sharpened. "She wants me dead?"

"Not yet."

Maris leaned forward. "But survival, Vivianne, isn't protection. It's permission. Temporary."

Another silence.

Then—Maris's tone shifted, husky and rich with memory. "I met Camellia in Kyoto. She was an assignment. A cipher with high clearance. I was to observe, extract data, and disappear. Cold. Surgical."

Her fingers brushed her knee. "But she wasn't just art. She was architecture. Elegant. Exacting. Beautiful like a blade crafted to reflect its victim's eyes. And beneath all of it—grief. Pressed and folded into her bones."

Her eyes softened, unfocused. "She moved like a cathedral. Full of silence and something holy. And when she looked at me—it wasn't as an operative. Not even as a woman. She looked at me like I was real. Like I wasn't made to vanish."

Vivianne leaned in.

Maris continued, slower now. "We unraveled in mirrors. Touched without talking. Everything unspoken, choreographed in heat and hesitation. And when I left—because I had to—she never begged. But the absence she wore afterward? That was love."

Vivianne sat straighter. Her tone was hushed. "She received a flash drive... we decrypted it together. Camellia's hands shook. Not from fear. From recognition. It held logs, photos, classified correspondences. Names erased from archives. Government contracts hidden behind art foundations and embassies."

She glanced at Maris.

"They weren't criminals. The Solé family was... exceptional. Artists, architects, diplomats. Raised under precision. Not cruelty—but something colder. Expectation. They weren't allowed to fail, or break, or bleed."

Maris's jaw tightened. "That's why she never stops. Why she never breathes unless she's winning."

Then, quieter: "I placed the flash drive."

Vivianne stilled. "You..."

"An order. Dhalia's. I didn't know what was on it. Just that it would fracture something. That it had to."

Vivianne stared. "And it did. It cracked her open."

Maris looked away. "That sin... I wear it still. Even now."

Vivianne hesitated. "The fire. The one Dhalia survived... it wasn't an accident."

Maris nodded. "No. It was a culling. Their grandmother's design. Dhalia was the one meant to die. But she lived—and everything after became a war she never stopped fighting."

The silence returned, dense as smoke.

"She blames Camellia," Maris said. "For forgetting. For living like the fire never touched her."

Vivianne turned slightly. "And she still haunts her."

"Every day," Maris murmured. "But that's not love. That's possession."

Their eyes locked.

"And you?" Vivianne asked.

Maris whispered, "I loved her. Love her. But we were written in ink that bleeds when touched."

"And now?"

Maris looked away, then stood. Her voice was low and frayed, but resolute.

"Now I do my job. I guard the truths she's not meant to carry yet. Even if they were the same truths that tore her apart. Even if I'm the one who helped rip them open."

Vivianne stood, slower. Her voice softened—but it didn't falter. "And I still believe in her. Even when it hurts. Especially then."

They stood there, still—bound not by trust, but by a name that had changed them both.

And beneath the streets of Paris, the Solé legacy waited. Ready to bloom and unravel, the woman bearing its name cracked louder than she dared admit.

The wine glass clinked too hard against the marble.

"Too hard," Camellia muttered, watching the wine glass settle against the marble.

She stared at the tablet, shoulders hunched, robe slipping off one shoulder, curls a storm across her brow. The flash drive sat beside the wine bottle like an accusation.

Her fingers hovered again.

Click. The same folder. The same photos. The same damn letter from a man who had died with too many secrets.

Estate fire: classified cause.

Cause of death: inconclusive.

Witness testimonies: redacted.

Her name—blacked out.

Dhalia's wasn't.

"Why you?"

A whisper.

"Why were you the one gone? Why was I left behind?"

She tapped deeper.

A contract. Scanned. Dated before the fire. Her grandmother's signature. A payment trail.

One name. Masked in code.

But the intent wasn't masked.

Target: Dhalia Solé.

Method: Arson. To be ruled an accident.

Camellia's breath hitched. "It was never meant to be me."

The glass cracked in her hand.

"She was supposed to die."

The document flickered.

"And they paid for it."

The wine glass gave, splintering in her grip.

Blood welled up between her fingers. She watched it fall to the floor. Slow. Precise.

"You burned her," she whispered. "And now you want to erase me, too?"

She didn't wipe the blood.

"Let them come. All of them."

The gallery was silent, its halls a cathedral of glass and curated shadows. Camellia moved barefoot across the polished floors, blood smeared on her palm like war paint, her breath ragged and shallow.

Paintings watched in silence. Sculptures brooded under skylights fractured by shadow. The air held a faint chill, but her skin burned.

Then—motion.

A figure stepped from the periphery, carved from shadow and light.

Alex.

Not tousled, not casual—immaculate. His black dress shirt clung just enough to suggest precision beneath restraint. Cuffs fastened, collar open. Amber eyes steady. Hair neatly parted, only the barest curl at his temple daring disobedience.

He stepped forward. Calm. Intentional. A slow gravity in the way he moved.

Camellia's pulse jumped.

He smelled clean. Subtle. A quiet blend of tobacco and cardamom, touched with something she couldn't name—but knew.

"You shouldn't be here," Camellia said. Her voice cracked like a match.

Alex tilted his head slightly. "And yet, here I am."

He didn't look at the blood.

He looked at *her*.

"You're unraveling," he said.

She let out a brittle laugh. "Am I?"

He came closer. One step. Another. Until the distance between them was a question.

"I'm still here," he said, low and smooth. "Not because of anyone else. Because I choose to be."

Camellia's breath caught.

He raised a hand—slowly—and brushed her curls from her face, knuckles grazing her cheek. It wasn't dominance. It wasn't seduction.

It was presence. Warm. Certain. Real.

His scent wrapped around her, and for a moment she closed her eyes— not to retreat, but to inhale him. As if the moment might stay longer if she memorized the way he *felt*.

"Sit. Please."

His voice was softer now. He guided her gently to a nearby bench, knelt before her, and retrieved a compact medical kit from beneath a display shelf.

Alcohol. Gauze. Salve.

She watched as he cleaned the wound, precise and wordless. The sting made her flinch—but only slightly.

"You don't always have to bleed alone," he murmured.

Her eyes met his. Searching. Suspicious. Wanting.

"Let me be what you need," Alex whispered. "Just tonight."

Unseen, unnoticed—every camera feed inside Galerie Solé flickered.

And somewhere in the dark, Dhalia watched.

Alex pressed a kiss to Camellia's wrist.

Not to seduce.

To anchor.

He became the man Camellia thought could free her.

Even if it meant destroying them both.

Camellia disappeared up the stairs without another word.

The bench was empty.

Alex stood in the quiet she left behind, staring at his own hands. The gauze was red. His breath unsteady. But his focus never wavered.

This was what she needed.

It's what he had *trained* to be.

A tool. A comfort. A mirror.

But not a ghost.

He moved through the gallery like a man navigating memory. Every slant of light familiar. Every hallway a page he'd read before.

And though the system feeds had been breached, though unseen access had returned to a distant source—he didn't know.

He didn't need to.

He followed.

She hadn't asked him to. That wasn't the point.

Camellia's door wasn't fully shut. He stepped through the frame without knocking.

She turned sharply, robe tied now. Defensive. Regal. Bleeding fury masked as grace.

"Are you following me now?"

Alex didn't answer.

She advanced a step. "You think because you kissed my wrist, you know me? That I'm yours to—"

He kissed her.

It wasn't desperate.

It was deliberate.

She stilled. Breathing hard against his mouth. But she didn't pull away.

She didn't pull away.

That was enough.

Not consent for more—just permission to stay.

Somewhere far from the gallery, behind walls colder than truth and quieter than death—

Dhalia was watching.

The game was working.

And Alex had just tightened the leash.

Even as he pretended it wasn't there.

Chapter Nineteen: Dhalia Ascends

The room was cold, but Dhalia was not.

She sat at the edge of a low velvet chaise, one leg crossed over the other, a robe of deep wine clinging to her frame like night's last breath. The curtains were drawn against a moonless Paris, the city trembling beneath her like a well-fed secret. Across the suite, an old gramophone hummed something mournful and slow—Liszt, perhaps. Or grief, orchestrated.

Her eyes were fixed on the screen in front of her.

Camellia.

The image flickered in grayscale—a delayed feed from the gallery, looping the kiss like a wound that wouldn't clot. Alex's mouth against her sister's. Camellia's breath caught between rage and surrender.

She didn't flinch.

She didn't blink.

She simply watched.

Then—fingertips ghosted along her shoulder.

Maris.

Fresh from the safehouse. Still dressed in black. But softer now. Her curls damp from a recent wash, lips parted slightly as if in prayer or apology. She knelt beside the chaise and pressed her cheek to Dhalia's thigh without asking.

"I came when you called," she said, voice breath-warmed silk. "I always do."

Dhalia reached down, threaded her fingers through Maris's hair, and exhaled slowly. "Because you remember who owns you."

Maris's breath caught—half ache, half answer. "And who I choose."

Dhalia pulled her upward—slow, guiding, hungry—and the kiss they shared wasn't sweet. It was old. Familiar. Like slipping into a crime they never stopped committing. Their mouths danced between surrender and strategy. Their bodies curved into silence.

Afterward, Dhalia leaned back and let Maris tuck herself against her side, heartbeat steady beneath Dhalia's hand.

"You'll help me dress," Dhalia said.

Maris nodded. "For him?"

"For the devil with brown eyes, yes."

The answer hung in the air, quiet and certain—a vow dressed as a whisper.

The gown was black velvet with slits cut high enough to promise danger and sleeves structured like armor. Dhalia wore it like a knife. Maris applied the lipstick—blood-red, matte—and fastened the earrings last, her fingers lingering.

"Are you going to kill him?" she whispered.

Dhalia smirked. "Not yet. Tonight, we collect."

"Data?"

"Prints. Voice samples. DNA, if he gives me that too."

"And if he doesn't?"

Dhalia looked in the mirror. "He will."

She didn't wait for affirmation. The next move had already begun.

Jules Devereux was waiting, glass in hand, at a private tasting room near the Marais. No cameras. No servers. Just a locked door, a firelit table, and a vintage meant for billionaires.

"You wore red last time," he said, eyes grazing her collarbone.

"And you pretended not to notice."

"Not pretending now."

They dined like rivals courting truce. Every laugh a transaction. Every brush of his hand a negotiation. Dhalia let her eyes soften, let her voice tilt into something alluring and unthreatening. She sipped when he sipped. Touched his hand with subtle warmth. Let him pour her another glass.

Her ring had a micro-transmitter.

Her clutch held an embedded print scanner.

And her body?

Still a weapon. Still a vault.

Later, as Jules leaned in to tell a story of blackmail and politics, Dhalia placed a hand on his chest and smiled. His laughter echoed low and smooth—perfect for extraction. Her ring pulsed once.

Recording.

Fingerprint.

Heartbeat.

Everything she needed.

And he never noticed.

Because men like Jules always believed they were doing the seducing.

Jules was pouring another glass when Dhalia's hand slipped over his wrist—just enough pressure to slow him, just enough heat to linger.

"Another night," she murmured.

He looked amused. "Leaving already?"

Dhalia rose in one fluid motion, black velvet cascading like a shadow that knew its power. She adjusted a single earring in the mirror beside the door. "I've tasted what I came for."

He leaned back, studying her. "Will I see you again?"

She glanced over her shoulder, smile razor-sweet. "You'll feel me first."

Then she disappeared into the dark—steps silent, data secured, no trace but perfume in the air and fingerprints buried in the folds of silk napkins.

Elsewhere in the city, beneath velvet shadows and deliberate silence, another woman answered the night with poise sharpened by purpose.

The study light stirred to life with a warm, amber hum.

Camellia entered barefoot—damp curls spilling over one shoulder, the tie of her black silk robe cinched with just enough care to invite notice. She moved like a memory conjured at midnight. A whisper of lavender trailed behind her, steeped in heat and sin.

Alex followed, slower. Alert. Wanting. Careful not to touch the moment too hard.

She paused beside the lacquered desk, fingers brushing the phone like an afterthought. One message blinked—no sender, no subject, marked in red. A warning dressed as silence.

She stilled.

Alex's eyes swept her body, but landed on her hands.

"You should rest," he said, though the rasp in his voice made the suggestion sound more like temptation than care.

"I'll sleep when I'm finished," Camellia murmured, not turning.

His gaze stayed on her. "With what?"

She said nothing. Let silence do what words couldn't—cut without sound. Then she finally turned, slow and deliberate.

"I need the room."

"Who sent it?"

Alex hadn't meant for it to sound like an interrogation. But it came out too sharp, too curious.

Camellia didn't look up right away. When she did, her gaze was steady—amused, but in the way a blade might find humor in skin.

"You ask questions," she said, her voice velvet edged with ice, "like someone who forgets how quickly doors close behind them."

He held her stare, pulse slowing—but not steady.

"Just looked… important."

Her smile sharpened.

"They always are. But important doesn't mean yours to touch."

She stepped closer—not fast, not loud. Just near enough that her presence became pressure.

"Be careful, Alex," she murmured. "Boys who read between my lines tend to disappear without a sound. Or a burial."

Her gaze dropped—his collar, his throat, the flicker of heat behind his restraint.

Then she tilted her head. A pause. A single breath passed between their mouths—not a kiss, just temperature, like a warning dressed as mercy.

Then—just breath against his lips. No kiss. Just temperature.

"Another time," she whispered, voice like silk strung tight over a blade. "If you remain… useful."

She turned before he could speak. And Alex stood there, pulse ticking in his jaw, hardened by tension he didn't quite know how to name.

Her words struck like velvet over glass.

The door closed behind him like a secret folding shut.

Camellia lowered herself into the chair at the console, spine taut. Her fingers hovered—then tapped the biometric lock with intimate precision.

The terminal awakened, its screen aglow with old code and deeper secrets. Only one other person had ever touched this machine.

Vivianne.

Elsewhere in Paris, the night opened like a vein.

Maris stood at the window, city light playing over golden-brown skin in flickers of fire and shadow. Her back—still, sculpted, breath held like ritual—spoke of patience forged in longing. She didn't turn when the lock clicked.

The door shut with a whisper.

Steel met silence and only the hush of velvet, remained.

Dhalia entered like a storm that already knew who wouldn't survive.

Dhalia said nothing. She didn't need to.

Maris began to undress her without a word. Her fingers moved with practiced ease, but there was no haste—only reverence wrapped in touch. She slipped the black velvet from Dhalia's shoulders slowly, letting it fall like water over skin kissed too long by moonlight. The gown whispered down her body, clinging for one last moment before pooling at her feet—less a garment removed than a promise unwrapped.

Skin met skin.

Maris didn't speak. She dipped her head and pressed a kiss to Dhalia's shoulder—soft, deliberate, and slow enough to linger in the skin. It wasn't hunger. It was reverence tinged with want. Her hands stayed after, trailing lightly down Dhalia's arms, not to claim but to remember—every curve, every breath, every ghost between them.

Dhalia's breath hitched—not from surprise, but from restraint. Her eyes stayed fixed ahead, lashes low, but her body leaned back just enough to feel Maris more fully. She didn't grant permission. She never had to. Maris knew the permission lived in the tension, in the way Dhalia didn't pull away.

Another kiss, lower now—closer to the pulse beneath her skin.

Then fingers. Slow. Steady. Brushing the last edge of fabric from her hips, palms grazing thigh and curve like they were learning her all over again.

Maris's breath warmed the space between them, a hush more telling than any confession. She leaned in again, slower this time, lips brushing the curve of Dhalia's neck. Not asking. Not claiming. Just... remembering.

Dhalia didn't stop her.

The discarded gown lay like a shadow at their feet, forgotten.

Maris's hands skimmed lower—over the line of Dhalia's ribs, along the dip of her waist. Her fingers trembled only once, betraying the storm beneath her practiced grace. Dhalia caught the hesitation with a slow exhale, her eyes never leaving Maris's.

"Still so obedient," she murmured, voice like silk torn down the middle. "Even now."

Maris didn't reply. Her mouth moved lower—slow, reverent. Over the hollow of Dhalia's collarbone, down to the rise of her breasts. Her tongue flicked just once, tasting the salt and sin of the woman who owned her in every way that mattered.

Dhalia's breath hitched—but she didn't close her eyes.

Control was always watching.

Maris slipped to her knees, but it wasn't surrender. It was ritual disguised as desire. Her lips pressed to the curve of Dhalia's hip, her hands parting her thighs with a familiarity that bordered on devotion. She kissed the inside of her thigh—slowly, deeply—then again, higher, until Dhalia's fingers tangled in her curls with a grip that said *now*.

And Maris obeyed.

The first touch of tongue to heat was soft. Testing. But it deepened with every stroke—measured, practiced, until Dhalia exhaled her first real sound. It wasn't a moan. It was a command disguised as breath.

"Don't stop."

Maris didn't. She moved like she was writing a love letter in secret. With lips. With tongue. With everything she could never say aloud.

Dhalia leaned her head back, throat exposed, the dim city light painting her in molten strokes. Her hands guided, pressed, then let go—trusting Maris to finish what she'd started.

The room blurred into scent and rhythm.

Maris's moan hummed against her, low and aching. Dhalia's thighs trembled. Her grip tightened. A gasp—sharp, delicious—cut the air as release crested inside her like a velvet wave breaking over glass.

She didn't scream.

She smiled.

And pulled Maris up by the jaw.

Their mouths collided, tasting everything. Salt. Heat. Victory. The kiss was wild, open-mouthed and starving, but not clumsy—two women who had danced this edge too many times not to know the shape of it.

When they parted, their foreheads pressed. Breaths entangled.

Dhalia whispered, "You're mine."

Maris nodded, lips slick, voice wrecked. "Always."

Outside, the Paris night didn't know it had been a witness.

But inside that room?

History had just turned on the axis of a woman's mouth.

Their breathing slowed before their mouths did.

Fingers tangled in damp curls. Skin slick with heat and something deeper. When it ended—if it truly did—silence curled around them like a final exhale. Dhalia lay still, her body a stretched flame across the sheets, the rhythm of Maris's pulse still shimmered between her thighs like heat waiting to bloom again.

The room trembled in its silence.

Then Maris shifted first—nuzzling against Dhalia's shoulder, lips brushing the salt-kissed curve with the reverence of someone returning from war. No need for words. Just the familiar ache of aftermath curling between them like smoke.

Dhalia exhaled, slow and deep.

"Come," she said, rising.

Not a command. A promise.

Their bodies unwound from the satin sheets like secrets uncloaked, steps soft against the cold floor. The door to the marble-wrapped shower eased open with a sigh of hinges. Steam rose like invitation, already waiting—

195

curling in ribbons of warmth and forgetting.

The water was running before they stepped in. Dhalia stepped in first, her silhouette refracted—blurred and divine beneath the rainfall stream. Maris followed silently, closing the door behind her with a soft hiss of suction.

Inside, they said nothing.

Not at first.

The water poured from the rainfall head in a steady cascade—warm, heavy, endless. It hit Dhalia's back first, tracing the valleys of her shoulder blades, sliding down the curve of her spine. She didn't flinch at the heat. She welcomed it. Maris watched her for a beat too long, then reached for the soap—unscented, elegant, the kind that melted slowly with heat and pressure.

As Maris stepped in behind her she lathered her hands. No hesitation. One hand rested at her hip, the other trailing up her ribs to the space between her breasts—lingering like a secret too sacred to speak. Skin to skin, thigh to thigh, mouth hovering just below Dhalia's ear.

Maris began to wash Dhalia.

Not like a lover.

Not like a servant.

Like someone consecrating something dangerous.

Neither spoke.

The sound of water was enough. So was the slip of lather between them, the way Maris washed Dhalia like she was erasing the memory of any man's touch. The black velvet had been armor. This was revelation. Vulnerability. Intimacy not performed, but devoured.

Dhalia tilted her head back, letting the water drown her face, eyes closed, breath slow. Letting herself be cared for without forfeiting power. Because in Maris's hands, power wasn't something surrendered—it was shared.

A moment passed. Then another.

Maris turned Dhalia gently beneath the water, so they stood chest to chest, mouth to mouth but not quite touching. Their foreheads met, wet and warm.

"I see you," Maris whispered, barely audible over the cascade.

Dhalia's eyes opened, dark and unreadable. "Good."

And that was enough.

Her fingers traced the line of Dhalia's spine, slow and meticulous, circling the base of her neck where power seemed to sleep. She washed her shoulders, her arms, her back—pausing only when Dhalia exhaled a sigh that wasn't quite content.

"You're quiet," Dhalia said finally, voice muffled by the steam.

"You were watching her again," Maris replied, gentle but unsparing.

Dhalia's lashes lifted, droplets clinging. "I always watch."

"She's not ready."

"She doesn't need to be. Not for what's coming."

Maris moved behind her now, washing her chest, her stomach, down to her hips—slowly, carefully. They stayed that way until the steam began to fade—until purpose slid back into their veins like silk gloves pulled on finger by finger. Their bodies slicked against one another, heat and skin, but the air between them had shifted. The heat lingered, but now it burned with purpose.

"Did you get what you needed from Devereux?" Maris asked.

Dhalia nodded. "Voice sample. Prints. Sweat from his glass stem. The bastard even kissed my hand—left a perfect trace along the ring."

Maris arched a brow. "And the laugh?"

"Immaculate. He thinks I'm just another indulgence. Exactly where I need to be."

Maris reached behind Dhalia, turning the water a few degrees hotter. "You'll take him down?"

"I'll peel his empire apart layer by layer. And when he looks into the void he carved for others, I'll be the last thing he sees."

Maris leaned forward and kissed her once—soft, soaked, reverent. "Then let me stand beside you."

"You already are."

They rinsed in silence. Steam ghosted across their shoulders, over their scars. Dhalia turned the water off with a deliberate twist, stepped out, and wrapped herself in black terry cloth.

Maris followed, dripping and beautiful, eyes still fixed on her like worship and warning combined.

197

Dhalia glanced toward the small control pad on the wall.

"Tomorrow," she murmured, "we start digging into the servers we mirrored from Jules's personal cache. Have Kenji review the AI render logs. Anything flagged with Solé or Camellia gets priority."

"And Alex?" Maris asked, toweling off her hair.

Dhalia's mouth curled. "He's almost there. She's letting him in."

Maris hesitated, then lowered her voice. "And when he's done?"

Dhalia's eyes flicked to her—sharp, gleaming. "We remind him, he still has a job to do."

Chapter Twenty: Thorns of the Crown

She had bled for control. Now it bled her back.

The message burned on the screen like a wound that wouldn't clot.

Camellia didn't move at first. Didn't blink. Didn't breathe.

Her reflection stared back from the glass—hazel-green eyes wide and shattered, the black silk robe slipping off one shoulder like memory trying to escape. Her fingers, still damp from the shower, trembled once before curling into a fist.

Then the scream came.

Not a sound.

A motion.

The chair went first—hurled across the study with enough force to crack against the lacquered bookshelves, shattering glass, splintering wood. Papers scattered like ash. Her breath caught in her throat, then broke free in a growl too animal to belong to someone so polished. So poised.

She wasn't poised now.

She was a storm. A siren flayed.

Camellia swept the contents of her desk onto the floor—crystal pens, art books, framed memories of curated joy. All of it exploded across the parquet like betrayal. She kicked the edge of the cabinet until her bare foot split at the knuckle—red blooming on black tile, unnoticed.

Vivianne was gone.

The thought hit harder than any bullet could. Not dead. Not hurt.

Worse.

Unreachable.

Her Vivianne—her silent compass, her spine carved in calm—had been taken. Ripped from her orbit like a star devoured by dark matter. And Camellia had felt it like amputation without anesthesia.

The screen still pulsed.

She turned back to it, chest heaving, curls sticking to sweat-slick skin. The message glowed in silence, as if daring her to read it again. She didn't. She knew it by heart now. Every syllable was tattooed on her bones.

Her hands, bloodied and shaking, gripped the edge of the desk.

"You brilliant, loyal fool," she whispered, voice cracking with grief, not scorn. "You should've told me. You should've let me protect you."

Her next breath trembled.

"Whoever took you… they think this makes them powerful?"

The temperature in the room dropped—not from cold, but from purpose. From the sudden stillness that comes before a slaughter.

"I will burn the city to find you."

A lamp went next. The gold-stemmed Baccarat piece she'd commissioned after their first victory. The one Vivianne had placed beside her reading chair—always turned on before Camellia ever entered the room.

It smashed like an oath broken on marble.

She slid to her knees—not from weakness, but from the weight. Her hands pressed against the floor, blood smearing across reflection-polished stone like the ruins of a queen's crown.

And then she laughed.

Low. Wet. Hysterical. A sound with no place in any cathedral but this one.

"Am I not still divine?" she spat, voice cracked and furious. "Does absence dethrone me? Does silence steal what I built?"

Camellia stood again, slow and shaking, dragging her pain upright like a flag. Her robe clung to her skin, exposing the swell of one breast, the red-streaked ankle, the bruises blooming like guilt beneath her ribs. She didn't care. She was beyond care. Beyond shame.

She walked to the wall and punched it—once, twice, until her knuckles sang hymns in crimson. The sound echoed through the penthouse like gunfire in velvet.

And still, the message waited.

Unread to anyone else. Unseen to the world.

But Camellia had read it.

And she knew—Vivianne hadn't just vanished.

She'd been pulled—ripped—from the inner sanctum of Camellia's world.

Not by doubt. Not by betrayal.

But by force.

The kind of violence that doesn't kick down a door—it *slips past the locks you thought only she knew.*

The kind that doesn't scream.

It whispers.

And leaves the crown bleeding.

Outside the penthouse, Paris remained indifferent.

Its streets pulsed with muted lights and muffled engines, unaware—or perhaps uncaring—that something sacred had fractured above them. Somewhere beneath that same city, beneath cobblestone and concrete and civility, a very different silence reigned.

Not the silence of grief.

But the silence that came before pain.

The hallway to the lower level was narrow—stone-choked and sound-proofed. Jules moved through it like a man descending into his own ribcage, hands tucked neatly behind his back, breath steady as wine before the spill.

The door at the end wasn't locked.

It didn't need to be.

Inside, the air buzzed.

Low, metallic hums. Sweat. Iron. A current that whispered promises in volts.

The room wasn't large, but it held more silence than a cathedral. The walls dripped faint condensation—soundproofing had a price. Two bodies occupied the center: one hanging, one bound.

The man—young, trembling, French-Algerian maybe—hung from a steel bar by his wrists, feet barely grazing the floor. His shirt had been removed, his chest streaked with the raw burn of electricity. Twitching. Gasping. A single black eye already blooming like rot.

The woman sat in the corner—restrained, gagged, ankles zip-tied to the chair. But her eyes were clear. Furious. Familiar.

Undeniable.

Vivianne.

Jules stepped closer, studying her face. Untouched. Unspoiled. The symmetry was exact. The poise. Even now, restrained and silent, she radiated that infuriating, exquisite stillness. *The calm in the storm.*

He smiled.

"Where did you find her?" he asked without looking at Luciano.

Luciano didn't turn either. He was across the room, barehanded for now, stripping off a stained leather coat and revealing a pair of black gloves—sleek, armored, and humming faintly at the knuckles. Each finger was capped with conductive studs, and a dial on the wrist gleamed like the eye of something watching. These weren't gloves. They were instruments—Luciano's signature. A dial on the wrist clicked as he turned it. He'd swapped the unit to constant-current, letting the machine dole out pain by milliamps instead of guesswork.

"Unmarked vehicle," Luciano said, voice calm and low. "Intercepted it six blocks out from the gallery. She didn't run. She stayed behind—like she expected to be collected."

"She didn't run?"

"No. She watched me approach. Like she wanted to be caught."

Jules finally stepped forward, crouching in front of her.

"You're very pretty," he murmured. "But that's not why I'm interested in you."

Her eyes flared. Even gagged, she radiated insult.

He smiled.

"You always were loyal to a fault, Vivianne. But even loyalty bleeds eventually."

The woman made no sound. No movement. Her stillness was deliberate.

"Why didn't you run?" he asked.

Her only answer was breath. Shallow. Controlled. Not panicked— calculated.

Luciano narrowed his eyes. He didn't expect her to break. Not quickly. But even silence could scream, if you leaned close enough.

He reached forward—not to hurt her, not yet—but to test the space between recognition and cruelty. His gloved fingers hovered at her temple, then brushed a curl behind her ear with surprising care.

"She always was the quiet type," he murmured.

Jules said nothing. He moved behind her, hand trailing along the back of the chair. Not possessive. Not intimate. *Invasive.*

"Vivianne," he said, voice almost warm. "You've been with Camellia for a long time. Long enough to know her soft spots. Her blind ones. So I'll give you a chance to return the favor."

Still no answer. Her gaze never left the mirror across the room—watching her reflection the way only someone trained to notice their surroundings does. No fear. Just calculation.

Luciano adjusted the dial on his gloves. The studs clicked.

"I'm going to ask again," Jules said, stepping back into her line of sight. "Tell me where she's hiding her intel. Where she's moving it. What names she's scrubbing from her gallery's files."

Silence.

"Start with him," Jules said softly, without turning. "She'll talk when she watches something she cares about scream."

Luciano's boots echoed as he approached the man. The hanging captive moaned—soft, guttural, from somewhere deep inside his broken ribs.

Luciano flexed his fingers. The glove tips sparked.

"As you wish."

The room hummed higher.

Luciano stepped into the dim circle of overhead light, rolling his shoulders beneath his tailored black shirt. The gloves hissed softly as he flexed his fingers—tiny blue sparks licking the air with anticipation.

The man hanging from the bar moaned again, head sagging low, wrists already raw and bleeding. His name was irrelevant. His screams were not.

Luciano reached for the jumper cables clipped to the edge of the car battery, the copper mouths already smeared with charred skin. He didn't rush. He adjusted the dial on the side of his glove with precise intent—20 milliamps per second. Enough to pulse. Enough to sting. Just shy of fatal.

He snapped the cables to the man's exposed sides—one at each rib. The body flinched hard, a wet, sudden jolt that arched his spine like a bow drawn too tight.

The man didn't scream yet.

Not yet.

Luciano didn't hesitate. He moved to the hanging man and struck him once across the ribs with the back of the gloved hand. Not to wound. Just to remind. Then—without ceremony—he pressed the charged knuckles to the man's bare stomach.

20 milliamps.

The man jolted, screamed, convulsed in the air like a marionette with its strings cut and rewired. His knees buckled uselessly below him. The sound echoed off the walls like a hymn from hell.

Jules smiled faintly, still kneeling before her. She blinked, once. Her throat moved around the gag, but she didn't look away. Didn't flinch.

Impressive.

"Do you know what makes electricity superior to fire?" Jules asked her conversationally, his tone as refined as ever. "Fire burns and disfigures. Electricity remembers. It imprints. Leaves the nervous system shattered, unpredictable. It rewrites pain."

The man sobbed now—high, pleading sounds between jolts of muscle spasms and shivering collapse.

Luciano removed the cables. Steam rose from the skin.

Then he slipped the glove off his right hand. Reached down. And gripped the man by the jaw—firm, unshaking.

Then he shoved two gloved fingers into the man's mouth—pressing hard against the tongue, the jaw, the soft roof.

The dial clicked upward.

35 milliamps.

The body seized violently. Drool mixed with blood spilled down the chin, sizzling faintly where it hit the metal collarbone plate Jules had installed for such encounters.

The man made a sound that wasn't quite human.

Luciano withdrew his fingers. The glove hissed as it cooled.

Vivianne flinched. Barely. A twitch in the corner of her eye. But Jules saw it.

"Ah," he whispered. "So you *do* care."

Luciano pressed the glove again, this time to the man's collarbone.

Another shock. Higher. More violent.

The scream peeled out of him, throat-shredded and wet.

Jules crouched beside her again, watching her profile as it twitched in restraint. Her jaw was tight. Her knuckles white where they gripped the chair's armrests.

"You think she'll come for you," he said, voice low. "Camellia. You think she'll tear the city apart when she finds out what we've done."

Jules's gaze was fixed on Vivianne.

"She won't," he continued.

Another shock. The man sagged like dead weight. Spit and blood foamed at his mouth.

Jules leaned in, breath brushing her ear. "The longer you're silent, the slower he dies. But you already know that, don't you?"

Still—no reply.

Jules rose, brushing imaginary dust from his sleeve. Then, without warning, he backhanded her across the face—once. Controlled. Calculated. Not enough to break anything. Just enough to test what cracked beneath silence.

Her head snapped to the side. Blood traced her lower lip.

She turned back, eyes shining with something defiant. Or dead. Or both.

"She's been trained," Luciano murmured, admiring it. "Street and private. Quiet as Camellia, twice as stubborn."

Luciano stepped back, slowly removing the glove from one hand. His skin beneath was unmarred. He flexed his fingers.

"She's holding out," he said. "But not because she's unafraid. Because she's prepared."

Jules rose, brushing a hand over her hair—still immaculate, still untouched, a final insult.

"Break the driver... completely," he said coolly. "Then we'll start mapping her voiceprint. Whether she speaks or not, we'll make her confess."

Jules looked back at the man. "One more time."

Luciano didn't reply. He reached for the cattle prod.

It lit with a deep blue hum.

And this time, when it touched skin the scream split open something ancient.

Meanwhile Dhalia watched from her pedestal, in a room swathed in shadow and low light, where that scream echoed again—

through a speaker the size of a coin.

Dhalia didn't flinch.

She simply watched.

The feed blinked once on the encrypted screen—stable, narrow, streaming from a micro-camera sewn discreetly into the second button of the decoy's blouse. The angle offered a fixed, slightly upward-facing view: grainy glimpses of floor tiles, boots pacing, gloved hands sparking at the edges of vision.

Sound bled through the tiny speaker—*a man screaming, another man laughing softly, and a familiar voice speaking cruelty in velvet tones.*

Jules.

Dhalia muted the audio. She didn't need the words. She knew the pattern of violence.

"They bought it," she said, coolly. "Hook, line, and electrode."

Maris stood behind her, towel-wrapped and silent, eyes on the screen as Jules's silhouette passed briefly across the feed's upper frame.

"They think it's her," Maris murmured.

"They do." Dhalia adjusted the resolution with a swipe of her finger, zooming in slightly—just enough to watch the sparks dance in Luciano's knuckles as they passed in and out of view. "He hasn't touched her face. Not yet. He wants her recognizable."

"Is the capsule working?"

"She hasn't activated it yet. Timing has to be perfect. Too soon and Jules will suspect a planted wound. Too late and the blood won't match the trauma."

The screen jolted—Luciano had likely struck the driver again, hard enough that the decoy flinched. The camera shifted slightly with the motion, jarring the image off-center before stabilizing.

"She's good," Maris said, arms folding across her chest. "Holding tension without overacting."

"She's not acting," Dhalia replied, eyes narrowing. "She's remembering."

Maris didn't ask what she meant.

Dhalia leaned back, fingers steepling beneath her chin as she studied the limited frame. Just movement. Glimpses of boots. Shocks of light. A blood splatter caught on the tile.

"She won't break," she said flatly.

"And the driver?"

"Disposable. He was pre-dosed with microdoses of Devil's Thread. Just enough to heighten the pain, keep his reactions authentic."

Maris exhaled slowly. "How long until Jules tries voice mapping?"

"Soon. And when he does, I want every return query from his system rerouted through the Zurich shell and bounced to Kenya. Get Kenji on the shadow-side protocol for all biometric queries. Anything he extracts gets tagged and logged in our node."

Maris moved, quiet and efficient.

Dhalia reached for her wine glass, watching as a gloved hand entered the frame again—Luciano's, from the angle. He was close to the decoy now. Likely speaking. The camera captured only the edge of his sleeve and the glint of voltage.

She muted the screen again.

Leaned forward.

"It's beautiful," she murmured.

Maris glanced over. "What is?"

Dhalia's mouth curved faintly.

"The look on a man's face... right before he realizes the woman in front of him isn't afraid."

Somewhere far above the screaming, beneath the weight of silence and glass, the woman who once wore the crown stood barefoot in blood and finally understood that power was not worn.

It was bled for. Thorn by thorn.

Epilogue: Obsession Blooms Where Love Dies

Dhalia's arms wrapped around her from behind—bare skin, breathless quiet, the scent of violets and vengeance still clinging to her collarbones. Maris didn't pull away.

She never did.

They stood like that for a long moment. In silence. In aftermath. In the ache of everything that couldn't be spoken without ruining it.

Then Dhalia whispered near her ear, voice silked in smoke.

"You intercepted the transmission from the safehouse?"

Maris stiffened—just slightly. "Yes."

"You're sure?"

"I rerouted the original packet. Embedded the false flag. Anyone tracing it will hit Zurich and die in the loop."

Dhalia turned her gently by the shoulders, gaze sharp as razors but laced with something almost soft.

"And Vivianne's message?" she asked, quieter now. "The one meant for Camellia?"

A pause.

Maris didn't blink. "It was altered before it left the node."

Dhalia studied her. Eyes dark. Bottomless.

Then she tilted her head—just enough to see into Maris, not past her.

"Do you love her?"

It wasn't an accusation. It wasn't even cold.

It was worse.

It was curious.

Maris didn't answer.

About the Author

D.J. Sumpter is an Army veteran, IT professional, and multidisciplinary artist whose true home lies in the written word. Their debut erotica suspense thriller trilogy, Twin Roses, is a masterclass in tension, seduction, and psychological depth—where art and identity collide in dangerous, unforgettable ways.

With a background as rich and varied as their characters, Dorian brings a lifetime of discipline, creativity, and introspection to the page. A former woodwind musician specializing in the saxophone, and a visual artist with a flair for evocative imagery, Dorian approaches storytelling with a cinematic eye and a musician's ear for rhythm and restraint. But it is in writing—especially in exploring the hidden motives and raw desires of complex characters—that they feel most alive.

Twin Roses follows Camellia and Dhalia—two women locked in a war of mirrors and seduction, tangled in shared history and divided by love, power, and control. Through rich prose and emotional precision, Dorian crafts a world where every glance is a threat, every touch a question, and every secret another step toward unraveling. The result is an intoxicating blend of erotica, suspense, and psychological intrigue, designed to make readers feel, ache, and think.

Influenced by themes of duality, trauma, obsession, and transformation, Dorian Sumpter's voice is both intimate and unrelenting—perfect for readers who crave stories that challenge as much as they arouse.

www.ingramcontent.com/pod-product-compliance
Lightning Source LLC
Chambersburg PA
CBHW020143120726
47903CB00007B/2384